“Natalie?” A bar
behind her sent

She knew that voice. Her legs threatened to give way. It couldn’t be. Her heart clamored. Her breath stalled as she turned in slow motion.

Lane Gray. In the flesh. A gentle spring breeze tousled his dark hair. His green eyes turned the deepest parts of her heart into mush and sapped all the moisture from her mouth. Butterflies took flight in her stomach.

As brain-dissolving handsome as ever. The first and only guy she’d ever loved. The one who’d broken her heart into tiny jagged pieces.

“What are you doing here?” Their voices blended together.

He flashed a heart-stopping grin. “The bride invited me. You?”

Wedding crashing for a glimpse of my daughter. She shrugged. “I know everyone in Aubrey.”

“You look great.”

Great! Nine years since she’d seen Lane and here she was in a blah dress—navy, high neckline, and the hemline barely above her knees—borrowed from her sister to crash a wedding unnoticed. Nothing she’d normally be caught dead in. Dressed more for a funeral than a wedding. *Her* funeral—if Wyatt caught her here…

SHANNON TAYLOR VANNATTER

is a stay-at-home mom and pastor's wife. Her debut novel won the 2011 Inspirational Readers' Choice Award. When not writing, she runs circles in the care and feeding of her husband, their son and church congregation. Home is a central Arkansas zoo with two charcoal-gray cats, a chocolate Lab and three dachshunds in weenie dog heaven. If given the chance to clean house or write, she'd rather write. Her goal is to hire Alice from the Brady Bunch.

SHANNON TAYLOR VANNATTER

Rodeo Regrets

ISBN-13: 978-0-373-48666-3

RODEO REGRETS

This edition published by arrangement with Love Inspired Books.

www.LoveInspiredBooks.com

Printed in U.S.A.

But if we walk in the light, as he is in the light, we have fellowship one with another, and the blood of Jesus Christ his Son cleanseth us from all sin. If we confess our sins, he is faithful and just to forgive us our sins, and to cleanse us from all unrighteousness.

—*1 John* 1:7, 9

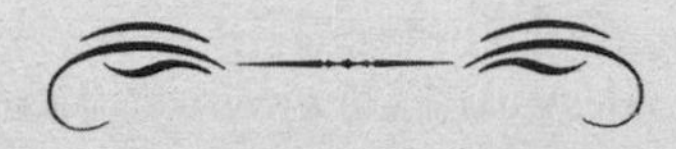

To my agent, Nalini Akolekar,
for helping me navigate the world of publishing.
You have a comforting spirit, and you always
make me feel better when we talk.

Acknowledgments

I appreciate DeeDee Barker-Wix,
Director of Sales at the Cowtown Coliseum, former
Aubrey City Hall secretary Nancy Trammel-Downes,
Aubrey Main Street Committee member
Deborah Goin, Aubrey librarian Kathy Ramsey, and
Steve and Krys Murray, owners of Moms on Main.

Chapter 1

Reduced to lurking behind a tulle-draped pillar, Natalie Wentworth's stomach did a flip-flop. Where was Hannah? Just a glimpse of her daughter was all she needed. Her first glimpse ever, though Hannah was eighteen months old now.

The early April sunset painted the big Texas sky in purples and pinks above the outdoor reception. A bright red barn provided background for the bridal party in denim and lace, with cowboys and cowgirls in full gear gathered in clusters laughing and eating. A few couples two-stepped to the twangy music. But no kids.

Wyatt had to be here somewhere. The newspaper said the bride and groom attended that church he'd tried to get her to visit back when she'd first gotten pregnant. And the groom was backup announcer at Cowtown Coliseum, Wyatt's stomping grounds.

A familiar swagger caught her attention. The dishwater-blond cowboy stopped at the dessert table. Wyatt. Her daughter's father. With a dark-haired woman. Natalie ducked farther behind the pillar. Why wasn't Hannah with him? Did the new woman in his life not like kids?

"Natalie?" A baritone voice directly behind her sent a shudder through her.

She knew that voice. Her legs threatened to give way. It couldn't be. Her heart clamored. Her breath stalled as she turned around in slow motion.

Lane Gray. In the flesh. A gentle spring breeze tousled his dark hair. His green eyes turned the deepest parts of her heart into mush and sapped all the moisture from her mouth. Butterflies took flight in her stomach.

As brain-dissolvingly handsome as ever. The first and only guy she'd ever loved. The one who'd broken her heart into tiny jagged pieces.

"What are you doing here?" Their voices blended together.

He flashed a heart-stopping grin. "The bride invited me. You?"

Wedding crashing for a glimpse of my daughter. She shrugged. "I know everyone in Aubrey."

"You look great."

Great! Nine years since she'd seen Lane and here she was in a blah dress—navy, high neckline and the hemline barely above her knees—borrowed from her sister to crash a wedding unnoticed. Nothing she'd normally be caught dead in. She felt as if she were dressed more for a funeral than a wedding. Her funeral—if Wyatt caught her here.

She had to get rid of Lane before he drew attention to her.

"So Nat, what have you been up to for the last nine years?"

Fun. With no strings attached. *You taught me not to let my heart get involved.* "I went to college, got my marketing degree, worked as the publicist for Six Flags Over Texas and just signed on as publicist for the Stockyards."

She tugged at her sister's demure pearl necklace. *Had a*

baby—here to see her, not you. And Lane Gray wouldn't blow it for her. "Don't let me keep you."

"Imagine that." He stepped closer to her. "Both of us back in Aubrey?"

Her breath caught. Aubrey wasn't big enough for both of them. Maybe the commute from Garland wasn't so bad, after all. But for the last eighteen months, she'd tried to forget Hannah. And her life had disintegrated. She couldn't sleep. She couldn't focus. She couldn't function.

If she could just get a glimpse of her little girl, maybe she'd be okay. Maybe she could get on with her life.

A woman carrying a baby, surrounded by toddlers, joined the gathering at the punch table. Clay's mom—always the designated babysitter. Was one of the children Hannah?

Natalie stepped closer to get a better look.

"Nice seeing you, too." Sardonic humor laced Lane's tone.

A redheaded girl—probably Clay and Rayna's. A boy. Natalie scanned another little girl. Dark hair, blue eyes, heart-shaped face. Just like her own. Hannah. Something in Natalie's chest exploded. She followed the toddler as if pulled by a magnetic force.

"Natalie." Wyatt stepped in front of her, blocking her path. "What are you doing here?"

She strained to see around him. Her eyes scalded. "I just wanted to see her."

"It's a bit late for that, don't you think?" His teeth clenched.

Why hadn't she stayed hidden, stuck with the plan for Wyatt to never know she was there? She'd wanted a glimpse of Hannah, but all other thoughts had flown from her head when she got that glimpse.

"Wyatt, what's wrong?" The dark-haired woman joined them. Her hair was a shade lighter than Natalie's and her eyes were a faded blue.

"You need to leave, Natalie. Now," Wyatt ordered.

"Natalie?" The woman's jaw dropped.

"Don't ruin Lacie's wedding day. You know what she's been through." Wyatt grabbed Natalie's arm.

She tried to pull away. He held fast, but he was gentle. Maybe he had changed.

"Let go of her," Lane growled from behind her.

"I'm just escorting her out. She wasn't invited."

"The newspaper said all friends and family welcome." Natalie's gaze stayed riveted on Hannah.

Wyatt's hand fell to his side. "You're not in either category and you know it, Natalie. This whole thing is a ploy."

"Wyatt, please." The dark-haired woman begged. "Don't cause a scene."

"Let me take you home, Nat." Lane offered her his arm.

"I have my car. And don't call me Nat." She spun on her heel and stalked away. Tears blurred her vision, but she held it together.

Go home alone and drown her sorrows in chocolate and tissues? No. She knew the perfect cure. But could she go through with it?

As she neared her car, movement in a pickup truck caught her attention. A girl and a boy in an intense embrace. She averted her gaze, until she heard a door open.

"Don't be mad, Jeff. I'm not sure." The girl stood outside the passenger side now.

Natalie ducked behind another truck. She didn't want to witness this scene or embarrass the teens. She just wanted to get out of here.

The boy got out of his truck and came around to the girl. He rubbed his hands up and down her arms. "Maybe I can convince you."

"If I leave, what if my mom starts looking for me? And besides, I don't think I'm ready."

"Huh?" His hand clamped on the girl's upper arm. "Listen,

Brittany, I don't know what kind of game you're playing, but you've led me on for weeks. And now you don't wanna play?"

With everything in her, Natalie wanted to stay hidden, to not get involved, but she couldn't let this brute manhandle the poor girl.

Nonchalantly, she stepped into view as if she hadn't been hiding. "Let go of her."

That deer-caught-in-the-headlights look passed over the boy's face before his Mr. Too Cool mask slipped firmly back into place. "Make me."

Back at the party, Lane shook his head. Natalie Wentworth. Still gorgeous after all these years. But her eyes were different, her expression pinched as if life in general hurt.

"I guess you *know* her?"

Did Wyatt really use the emphasis or did he just hear it that way? Lane's blood boiled. But he couldn't deny it. He'd been the first to *know* Natalie. "We went to school together."

"Watch your back with that one."

"You know—" Lane clenched his fists "—I never did like guys who dis women. Or grab them, for that matter."

Wyatt rolled his eyes. "I didn't hurt her. I just wanted her out of here before she ruined everything for Lacie and Quinn. And me."

"Come on." Wyatt's wife shot him "the look" and grabbed his hand. "This is my sister's wedding day. I need to see her off and help with the cleanup. We'll deal with this later."

Wyatt sighed. "Natalie and I bring out the worst in each other. But you're right. I had no right to touch her. And I should be praying for her instead of dissing her."

Lane relaxed his stance. "That's more like it."

The couple walked away.

What was that about? Why wasn't Natalie welcome at the

wedding? Why were things so tense between her and Wyatt? A past relationship?

A burst of laughter and shouts rang out behind him. He turned as the bride and groom ran through a shower of birdseed and escaped into Quinn's waiting pickup. The happy couple smiled and waved as Quinn drove away.

Lane jogged toward his truck. He'd had about enough happily ever after for one day. Lacie and Quinn were a nice couple, and they deserved happiness. But these days, weddings drove home everything he didn't have. Everything he didn't deserve. He'd hurt so many women in the past, including Natalie. He deserved to be alone.

But it still hurt, especially after seeing her again.

Natalie propped her hands on her hips as an engine started up on the other end of the parking area. "Sounds like the wedding's over and several dozen cowboys are headed this way. Within screaming distance. I said, let go of her."

"Gladly," the boy growled. He let go of the girl and stomped back to the driver's side. "She ain't worth it anyhow." The truck door slammed and the engine rumbled to life. The boy gunned it, spewing gravel in his wake as he careened down the drive.

"You okay?"

The girl rubbed her arms and nodded. "You're Mrs. Wentworth's daughter."

Natalie scanned the girl's downturned face. "Brittany Miller?"

The girl nodded again.

The last time Natalie had seen her, Brittany had been about six. In her mother's Sunday school class.

"Did you come with that guy?"

"No. My mom's the wedding planner. I invited Jeff so we could hang out. But he wanted me to leave with him and..."

Gravel crunched. Rapid footsteps. Natalie looked up and caught a glimpse of Lane headed in their direction.

She grabbed Brittany's arm and pulled her behind a pickup truck. "Shh." She pressed a finger to her lips.

Brittany frowned, but kept quiet.

Lane's footfalls neared. Way too close. Pulling Brittany with her, she inched around the truck and closed her eyes like she used to during hide-and-seek.

"Natalie?"

She opened her eyes to meet Lane's scowl. Her face heated.

"I hope you're not trying to sneak back in."

"No. I, um…I was just leaving."

"Really?" His left eyebrow cocked.

"Yes, after Brittany and I finish talking. I thought you might be Wyatt."

"Wedding's over. Won't be long before he heads this way. Probably best if you're gone."

"Right." But this was important. Wyatt would have to deal with it. "Let's talk in my car. Come on, Brittany." She turned to her bright blue Challenger, forcing her gaze away from Lane.

Brittany crawled in beside her. "Who was that? And why were we hiding from him?"

"Just someone I'd like to avoid."

Lane got into the truck they'd hidden behind.

Out of all the vehicles in the parking lot, she'd chosen his.

His engine started, and he backed out. Once his truck was out of sight, she started breathing again.

"And Wyatt?"

"You sure ask a lot of questions. Just someone else I'd like to avoid." She glanced at Brittany. "My turn. So you're dating that guy?"

"For two months."

"How old is he?"

"Eighteen."

It was none of Natalie's business, but the question buzzed in her head. "Is he pressuring you for sex?"

Brittany turned toward her. "How did you know that?"

"Been there, done that."

"I don't know if I'm ready."

"Then you're probably not. How old are you?"

"Sixteen. And a half."

"Have you ever?"

Brittany's gaze flitted away. "All the girls are doing it."

"Not all of them. Only the stupid ones."

Silence.

"I know you don't really know me, Brittany. But I've been where you are. If you haven't had sex yet—don't. Especially with Jeff. And if you've had sex with someone, stop now. You're too young. It's actually illegal at your age."

Brittany rolled her eyes. "Jeff is a nice guy."

"Yeah, I can tell." Sarcasm laced her tone.

"He was mad."

"If he cared about you, he wouldn't have gotten mad at you. Maybe frustrated, but he wouldn't have pressured you in the first place—if he cared about you."

More silence.

"Listen, Brittany. I know you think it's none of my business. But when I was your age, my boyfriend pressured me until our dates weren't even fun anymore." A boulder sank to the pit of her stomach. "Instead of resisting, I gave in. I thought if I gave him what he wanted once, he'd leave me alone and we could have fun again. But it only made him want more until that's all our relationship was about. And then he broke up with me."

"What did you do?"

"I dated someone else, but he knew I'd slept with my ex-boyfriend, so he said I had to prove I loved him by sleeping with him, too. So it went on and on." She glanced at Brittany again. "Don't set yourself up for going to a wedding and having to avoid half the men there because you've..."

The young girl kept her head down, but a blush swept up her cheeks.

Natalie reached over and patted her hand. "Don't get into that cycle. You don't even know what love is yet. And guys that age wouldn't recognize love if it bit 'em in the backside. All they want is sex—from whoever will give it up."

"I need to go find my mom before she realizes I'm gone." Brittany opened the car door.

"I hope you'll think about what I said."

"If you won't tell my parents about Jeff."

"If you'll promise to think about what I said."

With a nod, Brittany hopped out and hurried back toward the barn.

Natalie started her engine. She should take her own advice and go home. But she'd done her good deed for the day. And it had been too long since she'd had any cowboy comfort. At this point in her life, cowboy comfort was the only thing that kept Natalie going.

Country twang, neon lights and drunken, dancing couples. The perfect blond, buff and bronze cowboy sat in the booth beside Natalie. The perfect cure for what ailed her.

She closed her eyes and tried to lose herself.

A rough hand clamped on her bare knee. "Hey, babe, let's get this party started. Your place or mine?"

Bile rose in her throat. She swallowed and picked up the untouched strawberry daiquiri he'd bought her. The whiff of alcohol brought the bitter taste into her mouth. She set the glass down.

Her words of wisdom for Brittany haunted her. Stop the cycle. Was it too late for her? Her chin trembled.

"Uh." He scrubbed his fingers over his stubbly beard. "You gonna cry or something? I'm not looking for anything heavy. Just a little fun."

Fun. Exactly what she needed. To forget her cares and worries in this guy's arms. But she couldn't do it.

"I'm sorry. I can't." She shivered and slid out of the booth.

The man followed, grabbed her and pulled her against him. "Maybe I can warm you up."

She pushed away from him. "I don't even know your name."

"Does it matter?"

"I've changed my mind."

"It's a bit late for that." His hand clamped on her wrist, his fingers biting into her skin.

"I'm feeling sick. I have to go."

His grip on her wrist tightened, and then he flung her away from him.

She stumbled, her stiletto turned. Sharp pain shot through her ankle, but she caught herself.

"You best watch who you mess with, lady," the cowboy growled. "You could get yourself in a heap of trouble toying with the wrong man."

"Is this guy bothering you?" A deep voice thundered over her left shoulder.

"No. I was just leaving." Natalie turned to see her would-be rescuer.

Mitch Warren. Her sister's high school sweetheart.

"Natalie?" His eyebrows rose.

"Hi, Mitch." Straight-and-narrow Mitch. Texas Ranger Mitch. "What are you doing here?"

The cowboy stalked back to the booth they'd abandoned.

"Let's just say—" he lowered his voice "—I'm on duty."

"Oh."

"Listen, Natalie, this isn't the kind of place you should hang out in. I've made a lot of arrests here."

"I'll keep that in mind."

"Need a ride home?"

"No, I've got my car, but thanks."

"I'll at least walk you out and make sure Marlboro Man doesn't follow." Mitch stared into her eyes. "You haven't been drinking, have you?"

"Not a drop. Scout's honor." She blew in his face.

A smile cracked his cop mode and he offered his arm. "Let's get you out of here."

Mitch hustled her outside to her car. She unlocked it, slid in and lowered the window.

"Make sure it starts okay."

She turned the key and the engine caught.

Mitch leaned his elbows in her open window. "How's Caitlyn?"

"Okay. Her two clothing stores keep her busy."

He nodded. His mouth tightened. "Tell her I said hi."

"I will."

"And, Natalie, don't let me see you around here again. It's beneath you." He patted the car and stood watch as she pulled away.

Mitch had tried to do for her what she'd tried to do for Brittany.

The headlights of her lone car illuminated the abandoned streets of Aubrey, but Natalie didn't remember driving here. Had she stopped at red lights? Stop signs?

What was wrong with her? Was she going crazy? She'd left the cowboy at the bar.

Considering his reaction to her refusal, maybe that was a good thing.

Natalie touched the raw skin on her wrist and shivered

despite the seat warmer. But now she'd spend her first night back in Aubrey alone. A cowboy would have been much better than tissues and chocolate.

Not so long ago, it had all been a fun game when she was bored—or lonely. Go to a bar, get drunk, take a nameless cowboy home. But now it turned her stomach.

If Mitch hadn't shown up, would the cowboy have followed her?

Her engine stuttered. Her gaze flew to the gas gauge. Well below the *E*.

"No. No. No." Just what she needed to top off this horrid day. She slammed her open palm against the steering wheel. The sting of the blow throbbed through her hand.

The engine choked and coughed, then died. She blew out a sigh, coasted to the shoulder of the road, and laid her head on the steering wheel. Drawing in a big breath, she flipped on the dome light and dug in her purse for her iPhone. Her hand clamped over the smooth, familiar shape. She jabbed the screen. Nothing. Great. She'd forgotten to charge it. Again.

She opened the door and stepped out into the night air. Though the temperature had been in the seventies today, the evening had cooled to the low fifties. The skimpy little black dress she'd changed into after the wedding didn't help much.

Stars spangled the big Texas sky. The lights of Aubrey glowed in the distance. No traffic at midnight. She'd walk to the old farmhouse at the edge of town. It had been empty for a few years, but evidently someone lived there now. Probably someone she or her parents knew. Everybody knew everybody in Aubrey.

Caitlyn would come get her from there. No questions asked between sisters. She'd have to come up with a little white lie to cover where she'd run into Mitch. Or maybe she shouldn't mention it. Caitlyn was still nursing Mitch-inflicted wounds from ten years ago.

She hugged herself and trudged along the shoulder of the road illuminated only by the moon. At least it was still too cool for rattlesnakes.

The little black dress had done the trick tonight—attracted a cowboy as she'd planned. Why couldn't she go through with it? Because she was sober?

The smell of alcohol had turned her stomach ever since she'd gotten pregnant. And it couldn't be that again; she'd lived like a nun since her pregnancy. For too long. She'd needed a cowboy to help her forget. About Hannah. About Wyatt. About Lane.

A dog barked. She froze.

Something scurried through the field to her right. She bolted.

The dog barked again and a cacophony of canines joined in.

She could see the house now and charged toward it.

Her breathing ragged, she cut across the yard, turned her ankle again, and felt her way up the unlit porch steps. A low growl, deep and menacing, stopped her in her tracks.

The dog growled again, then barked from the porch. It sounded big. She backed down the steps. Her heel caught. She gasped and fell back, sprawling in the cool grass.

Light blinded her. She shielded her eyes with one hand.

The door moaned as it opened.

"What is it, Barney?" A gruff voice. A huge man with bulging muscles framed by the open doorway. Wearing a ribbed undershirt and basketball shorts, he ran his hand through sleep-tousled dark waves. The dog growled again.

Natalie shivered. Her eyes adjusted to the porch light. A rottweiler. A huge, backlit man. Had she gone from simmer to inferno?

"Barney, heel." The baritone was less gruff now. "Hey, you okay?"

That voice again. For the second time in one day. *Move,*

feet. Run before he recognizes you. Awkwardly, she tried to stand, but her ankle gave out.

"Natalie, is that you?" Lane opened the screen door.

Too late. It was too much—seeing Lane at the wedding, the confrontation with Wyatt, advising Brittany not to end up like her. Then the cowboy, Mitch's stern advice and her ankle. Punctuated with the dogs and Lane again to top off the evening. Tears stung her eyes.

"Hey. Are you hurt?" He took the steps in one leap. He knelt beside her and his hands settled on her shoulders.

She shuddered.

Lane helped her up and pulled her into his arms.

The arms she'd dreamed of for nine years. She pressed her face into his solid chest. He smelled like Irish Spring soap and sleep.

"Nat, you okay?"

Chapter 2

"I'm afraid of dogs," she sobbed against his shoulder. Like a complete ninny.

"What happened?"

"Just let me call Caitlyn."

"Not until you calm down and tell me what happened. This seems like more than a dog." He didn't say anything else, just held her.

Her life kept getting better and better. It would be worth it to commute to work from her apartment in Garland just to avoid him. She didn't have to live here.

But she was tired of her self-inflicted exile. Tired of hiding in shame. And she wanted to see Hannah again. Up close. The glimpse of her daughter at the wedding had only made her want more. If she could find closure where Hannah was concerned, maybe she could pull herself together.

She reluctantly stepped back from him. Striving to be casual, she patted his shoulder. Firm muscle. She jerked her hand away. “Sorry, I got your shirt soggy, but it sounded like a whole pack of dogs.”

“You gonna tell me what happened now?” Gently, he took her hand.

The rottweiler took a step closer.

“Is he safe?” Her hand trembled in Lane’s.

“Barney, in your house.”

The dog wagged his tail and headed for his doghouse.

Lane led her inside. The living room was neat, masculine and functional—except for one corner filled with tools, paint cans and a kitchen cabinet. Lane was remodeling. In for the long haul.

“Sorry for the mess. I gutted the kitchen and it’s slow putting it back together.” His gaze settled on the red mark around her wrist where the cowboy had grabbed her. His eyes narrowed.

“Just let me use your phone.” Her voice cracked. “I’m fine.”

“I’ve seen fine, and it doesn’t look like this.” He turned her wrist over. “Sit down and tell me who did this to you.”

She sank into the man-sized taupe couch and scrubbed her hand across her eyes. “Some guy at the bar. He got a little rough when I refused his ride home.”

He stiffened. “How rough? Who was it? Maybe I should pay him a visit. Or call the police.”

The police were already there. She shook her head. “I didn’t get his name.”

“Where’s your car?”

“I ran out of gas an eighth of a mile or so from here.”

“You walked from there? In those shoes?” He sat beside her.

“It was no big deal. Except for the dogs.”

His arm came around her shoulders.

She pulled away. “Just let me use your phone.” She sounded scared—weak—even to her own ears.

Why couldn't she pull it together? Pretend she was self-sufficient. Self-sufficient enough to remember to buy gas and charge her iPhone. Pretend she hadn't thought about him in years.

"I've got a gas jug," he said.

"Leave it. The car's well off the road. I'll call Caitlyn to come get me and we'll worry about my car tomorrow." She shrugged. "It's not like it'll get towed—or stolen—in Aubrey."

"You headed to your folks' place?"

She blew out a big sigh. "Actually, I'm headed to the house my parents built for me next door to theirs."

"I'll take you."

"That's not necessary."

"Why wake Caitlyn this time of night when I'm already up?" He stood and grabbed his keys from a table near the door.

Out of options, she followed. "Sorry for waking you so late." Why hadn't she agreed to let him put gas in her car? Now she'd be stuck in his truck. With him.

"Not a problem." He opened the door and waited for her to step through.

"Um, is Barney on a chain or anything?" Her voice was tremulous.

"He's harmless as long as I'm around or he knows you."

"Still I…"

"Let me put him in the backyard." He strode toward the rear of the house. A door clicked open, then closed. "Barney? Come here, boy." His faint voice, outside.

She scanned her surroundings and saw dark wood floors and walls, splashes of Southwest patterns for accent, and a huge flat-screen television.

A few minutes later, the door opened and closed again. Lane strode back into the living room. "There. Safely inside the fence."

"Thanks."

He threaded his fingers through hers, and she limped a few steps alongside him.

"You're hurt."

"I turned my ankle a little, that's all."

"Here, lean on me." He settled her arm around his waist, nestling her against his side.

She trembled. "Are there any other loose dogs around?" Please let him think she was uneasy about dogs instead of his nearness.

"I'll protect you. I promise." He supported her weight down the porch steps, all the way to his truck, and opened the passenger door for her.

She climbed in, feeling safer than she had all night. But she had to remember who Lane was. More dangerous than any rottweiler.

Lane's engine rumbled to life and he snuck a glance at Natalie.

She leaned back against the headrest. Vulnerable and tired. But at least she wasn't crying anymore.

Thank You, Lord, for letting me be here to help her.

What might have happened to her if he hadn't been around? His insides quivered. "Do you go to bars often?"

"What I do is none of your concern." Her voice shook.

"Maybe not. But it could be dangerous." His words were sharp.

"Listen, I appreciate your help, but if I want to take some cowboy home from a bar without even learning his name, it's my business. Got that?" Anger sounded in her tone, not tears.

Lane's stomach bottomed out.

Natalie had every right to hate him. But did she really take men she didn't know home with her? And if so, why hadn't she tonight? Because the guy got rough? Or had she made up the whole thing to dig at him?

"You should be more careful." Lane glanced her way. Please let her be making up the scenario.

"My drive's coming up on the left. Right before my parents' place." She pointed. "Right here. I could have walked the rest of the way. But the dogs—"

"No need to walk, and I'm glad to help." Natalie Wentworth, a mere mile down the road from his house. He turned into the drive. The road took him to a dollhouse. Just like her parents' place.

He killed the engine, got out, and came around to open her door. He offered his hand, but she didn't take it and climbed down from his truck without help. She winced when the weak ankle bore her weight, but with a determined set to her jaw, she didn't limp.

He fell into step beside her. "I've thought a lot about you over the years."

Sarcasm laced her laugh. "Yeah, I bet." She stopped and faced him.

"Really, Natalie." His hand cupped her cheek. "I mean it. I'm sorry for the way I treated you back then. You deserved better."

She stepped back. "No biggie. I'd forgotten you existed."

His hand dropped to his side. "I hope I didn't do this to you. Make you this hard."

"You give yourself way too much credit." She stalked away.

He waited until she was safely inside before driving away. Had he done this to her? She'd been innocent until she ran into him. Did she make a habit of leaving bars with nameless men she'd just met?

Oh, Lord, forgive me. Please keep her safe. In spite of herself.

Finally, Monday. Work. Exactly what Natalie needed to keep her mind occupied.

She propped her hands on her hips and scanned the store,

while her sister helped a young woman with her purchase. Twangy country music played in the background. Not loud enough to create distraction, just a nice ambience. It was a step in the right direction, but the maze of overflowing racks had to go. Caitlyn had stayed away too long. Left the care of her store—her baby—to another.

Figuratively, instead of literally, as Natalie had.

Her heart hitched.

Concentrate on the store. No wonder sales were down. Caitlyn's store would never get the rodeo contract at this rate.

But the location—right in the middle of the Fort Worth Stockyards—was priceless. Streamlined, appealing, top-of-the-line cowboy gear. Natalie would have it in shape by the end of the week if her sister would listen to her.

Once she saw Hannah again and got all the businesses in order, she could submit her publicity plan and work from Garland. Return to her no-worries life, without seeing Lane.

But after the wedding the other night, then happening upon his house and the ride home—her heart hadn't returned to a normal beat yet.

The bell over the door jingled as the customer left with a large bag.

"Okay, I'll admit my store got out of hand while I was busy opening the one in Dallas, but do you really think it needs that much work?" Caitlyn sounded nervous at the prospect.

Bless her heart, Caitlyn had always been a small thinker. Content with her rinky-dink store, when it could be so much more. She'd never have opened the second store if Natalie hadn't pushed her.

"Definitely, but we'll have our work cut out for us. I think a clearance sale is in order so we can bring in more upscale lines."

"That sounds expensive." Caitlyn nibbled her lip.

"If you get the contract, you'll have plenty of funds."

"Really?" Caitlyn's eyes lit up.

Maybe she would catch Natalie's vision.

The bell above the entrance jingled. From her spot near the register, she could barely see around the racks as a woman carrying a small girl managed the obstacle course.

"Welcome to The Sassy Cowgirl/Rowdy Cowboy. May I help you?" Caitlyn asked.

"We need new boots and we thought Aunt Cait was the perfect person to come to." The woman stepped into view with Hannah in her arms.

Natalie gasped. The woman who'd been with Wyatt at the wedding.

"Oh, I didn't realize that was you." Caitlyn's eyes widened and she reached for the little girl. "Hey, sweetpea."

"Me want pink." Hannah proclaimed.

Caitlyn stepped around a rack and shot Natalie a get-lost glare. "Well, let's see what we can find."

Natalie's gaze glued itself to Hannah's dark hair, which was braided in pigtails with a pink bow in each. The little girl's blue eyes mesmerized her, and Natalie's stomach took a dive. Her arms ached to hold her little girl. The reason she'd stayed away so long. Because she'd known if she actually saw Hannah, she'd never be the same.

Caitlyn zigged between two round racks, then zagged past another. "Excuse the mess, Star, but I'm rearranging some things. We'll be getting lots of new lines in a few days."

Star. How serious were she and Wyatt?

"These are pretty." Star grabbed a pair of lavender boots from the shelf.

"Me want pink." Hannah shook her head.

She definitely had her own opinion.

"I like pink, too. How about this?" Caitlyn nabbed a tiny pink pair.

Hannah's eyes lit up. "Pwetty."

Star put the lavender boots back.

"These were going on the clearance rack." Caitlyn wiggled the boots onto Hannah's feet. "I'll give you twenty-five percent off if they fit."

"You don't have to do that. Just treat us like any other customer."

"I need to move some merchandise, so it's no problem." Caitlyn set Hannah down and gently mashed the toe of each boot. "Plenty of growing room. Walk around and make sure they fit."

Hannah walked the aisle toward Natalie with a shy smile.

Her heart took another dive.

"How do they feel? Do they hurt anywhere?" Star hovered.

"They feel pwetty."

"Great." Caitlyn stepped over to the cash register and shot Natalie a why-are-you-still-here frown. She rang up the purchase and quoted the total.

Star hugged Hannah. "Since they're on sale, do you want a dress, too, Hannah?"

Ingratiating herself into Hannah's life by spoiling her. Natalie sank to the stool behind the register.

Hannah pointed to a pink frilly concoction. "This one."

"Very pretty. You have excellent taste." Star sifted through the rack, found the right size and set the dress on the counter. Her gaze shifted to Natalie and recognition dawned in her eyes. Star clamped her hand to her heart. "Oh. I didn't see you."

Caitlyn acted as if everything was fine. She scanned the dress and accepted the debit card Star handed her.

Natalie focused on the card and read the name imprinted on the shiny surface.

Star Marshall.

Natalie closed her eyes. Wyatt Marshall had married. Her daughter was being raised by another woman.

Caitlyn completed the transaction. "You still bringing Hannah over tomorrow evening?"

"We are. Hannah's excited about it." Star signed the receipt and looked up at Natalie. "You won't be—"

"No." Caitlyn shook her head. "Natalie won't be there. We'd definitely check with Wyatt on anything like that." Caitlyn pressed a kiss on Hannah's forehead. "See you then, Hannah. Bye-bye, sweetpea."

"I think we're just in time to watch the cattle drive before lunch." Star walked toward the door, but Hannah stared back at Natalie over Star's shoulder.

The bell jingled and the door shut behind them.

"You okay?" Caitlyn touched her shoulder. "When did you figure out who she was?"

"It's not the first time I've seen her. I crashed Lacie's wedding last week." Her eyes locked with Caitlyn's. "Why didn't you tell me Wyatt got married?"

"I figured it would only upset you."

"You see her?" Natalie's voice cracked. "Often?"

"Star brings her by Mom and Dad's a couple of times a week for a visit. Hannah calls them Grammy and Grand. She's a doll."

"Yes, she is." A doll Natalie could never hold.

Big breath. In and out. Calm, cool, collected. Natalie sashayed her hips in perfect, practiced rhythm as the heels of her fringed aqua boots clicked off each step across the brick-lined street. Thank goodness her ankle had recovered over the last week. She never thought she'd set foot in the Fort Worth Stockyards again. At least she wasn't limping in.

But it was her job now. An endless lineup of Friday- and Saturday-night rodeos. She wouldn't have to attend every one, but she had to frequent Cowtown Coliseum to get a feel for publicity angles. And she'd need to pop in regularly to survey the crowd, watch for an increase or decline in numbers once her plan was in place.

Besides, Wyatt would be here. Maybe she could talk sense into him. Maybe he and Star would have Hannah with them.

She shook her head. What was she thinking? He wouldn't bring Hannah to the rodeo. Not until she was older. Natalie hugged herself.

At the entrance of the Coliseum, she paused. Took one more deep breath. She showed her staff pass to the man at the door and stepped inside the lobby.

"Nat?" Lane called from directly behind her.

She turned around slowly. "Lane." His name came out all breathy. She clenched her teeth. "It's Natalie. Not Nat." He'd lost the right to call her by a nickname.

"Sorry." He held both palms toward her. "You look great."

"Thanks." At least he was right on that. Much better than the disaster she'd been at his house last week. In aqua, sparkly and curvy from head to toe, she was dressed to attract the perfect cowboy.

But not this one. His dark hair winged out from under his gray cowboy hat, begging her fingers to smooth it into place. "Why are you here?"

"I'm the new pickup man."

She arched her left brow at him. Was that some kind of line?

"For the broncs and bulls."

Oh. Rodeo. Why did his presence freeze her brain?

"You coming in?"

"I need something to drink first." A beer. Her stomach turned. She needed to keep a clear head anyway, so she'd get a tea, instead. She headed to the concession stand.

"I'm glad we're both back home." He matched her stride. "Maybe we could have dinner sometime?"

Her steps stalled. "Why?"

"I don't know. For old times' sake."

"Old times' sake is something you want to remember. I think I'll pass." She strode away, head held high.

At the concession stand, she leaned on the counter for support. *Don't follow me. Don't follow me. Don't follow me.*

She got her tea and turned around. No sign of him. She hurried inside the arena.

And smack into a hard chest.

"Whoa. Easy there, cowgirl." Lane's arms felt at home—around Natalie.

She jerked away from him. Fire blazed in her blue eyes.

"Just trying to make sure you don't fall for me." He shot her his most charming grin.

But it came nowhere near extinguishing the flare of her temper. His fingers itched to touch her long, dark hair. He shoved his hands in his pockets.

"Just stay out of my way." She sidestepped him and stalked around the walled walkway of the arena.

She was even more beautiful than she'd been nine years before. A woman instead of a girl. A woman who obviously regretted her past with him.

As he did. She'd been the only girl who'd ever told him no. Until he'd finally worn down her resistance. She'd given him everything, and he'd broken up with her. Used her and moved on to the next willing girl. He'd been such a jerk back then. If only he could have a do-over.

Since he'd become a Christian he regretted all the women in his past, even though they'd been willing. But Natalie had given in only because he'd pressured her. Somehow, hurting her had always haunted him, even before he knew Christ.

Natalie stopped at a box seat near the bull chutes and spoke to a cowboy. Lane was too far away to tell who the guy was, but his heart gave a painful lurch.

Jealousy? Why? He hadn't seen her since high school. He wanted her to be happy.

But with him, not some other guy.

Stars shot off in his head.

He loved her.

The vivid blue eyes that reached into his soul. Her laughter and sense of fun. The vulnerability she tried so hard not to let show.

He'd always loved her. That's why he'd regretted hurting her. That's why he'd broken up with her. Because she was the only one who touched his heart, and back then it scared the life right out of him.

Brain on the rodeo. He forced his gaze away from Natalie and hurried toward the arena. But as he neared the box seats by the gate, a woman stood up and tried to squeeze between Natalie and the glaring cowboy. Wyatt and Star.

"You could have at least told me you were getting married." Natalie's voice shook. "Especially when it affects our daughter."

"The daughter you didn't want." Wyatt's words cut through her heart. "The daughter you wanted to abort. The daughter you gave up."

"Please. Not here." Star pressed a hand against Wyatt's arm. "Can't we discuss this calmly and in private?"

"It's not my doing." Wyatt splayed both hands. "Natalie's the one that always has to make a scene."

Natalie rolled her eyes. "If I'd have stopped by or called, where would that have gotten me? I have to try to talk some sense into you whenever I get the chance." She counted to ten. "She's still my daughter. And I should know about any big changes in her life. Like her father getting married and some other woman raising her."

"Another woman has raised her from the beginning," Wyatt

growled. “My sister, my mom, even Caitlyn—up until Star and I married. You wouldn’t even look at Hannah in the hospital, so why should you care?”

Natalie’s eyes stung. “Well, I’ve seen her now, and I do care.”

“You don’t have any rights to her, Natalie. You signed all rights over to me. So whatever happens in Hannah’s life is no concern of yours.”

“Let’s meet somewhere and talk.” Star again. In her sweet little voice. “In a few days, after everyone calms down.”

Could anyone really be that nice? Maybe it was an act.

“There’s no reason to meet about anything.” Wyatt clamped his cowboy hat on his head. “Star adopted Hannah. Star is Hannah’s mother, legally and in our hearts. So just go back to Garland and leave us alone.”

Her heart lurched. She scanned Star. Her daughter’s mother? How could another woman adopt Hannah without Natalie even knowing about it?

“She’s my daughter. Even though you found a pale imitation of me to play house with.” She delivered the jab in a stone-cold tone.

Star’s sweet little mouth dropped open. “Were you attracted to me ’cause I look like her?”

“Don’t be ridiculous.” Wyatt drew Star against his side. “Trust me, dark hair and blue eyes are the only thing y’all have in common.”

Natalie’s heart sank. She’d meant to hurt Wyatt. Not Star.

“Natalie. You all right?” Lane asked, from over her shoulder.

Why did he keep sneaking up on her?

Her vision blurred. She had to get away. Before the tears fell. She whirled around and sidestepped him, then bolted around the arena and through the lobby.

“Natalie, wait!” Lane called.

Don’t follow me. Don’t follow me. Don’t follow me.

* * *

The bright sunshine momentarily blinded Lane, but he caught up with her. She was quick, but no match for his longer legs.

"Leave me alone." Natalie snapped.

"Not when you're upset." His stride matched her shorter one.

"I'm fine."

He turned her to face him. "No, you're not. I wish I didn't have a rodeo to work so I could take you home."

"I can drive."

"At least sit down a minute. Let's get you calmed down before you get behind the wheel." He led her to a wooden bench between the Coliseum and the fake bull ride.

"You'll be late for your rodeo." She sank onto the seat.

Lane checked his watch and settled beside her. "I've got time." Not much, but he couldn't leave her like this. "Wanna talk about it?"

"No."

He fished a tissue out of his shirt pocket.

"Thanks." She swiped at her eyes and blew her nose.

Completely vulnerable. Had she been hurt like this when he'd broken up with her?

"Come here." He reached for her.

She scooted away. "I'm fine."

"Yeah, I've seen your fine before."

Her laugh came out watery. "Couldn't you at least leave me the dignity of only seeing me when I look presentable, so you can at least regret dumping me?"

He laughed. "Trust me. I do regret that." And she still looked hot. Even hotter without her tough shell.

"Good."

"I take it Wyatt's an ex-flame?"

"It was nothing."

He tipped her chin up with gentle fingertips. “This looks like something.”

“It’s not about him. Trust me.” She dabbed her eyes. “I’m okay now.”

“You sure?”

“Positive. Don’t you have somewhere to be?”

“I’m different, Nat. I’m not the jerk I used to be. I’m a Christian now. I only want to help you. Maybe you could come to church with me sometime.”

She snorted. “Aren’t you the guy who pressured me into sex when I was sixteen? And now you’re some Holy Roller?”

Her words stabbed his heart. That’s probably how it looked to her. “I’m not a Holy Roller, just a sinner saved by grace.”

“Whatever.” She rolled her eyes.

“Why do you do that?”

“What?”

“Lash out when you’re hurt.”

“Let’s get one thing straight, Holy Roller.” She jabbed a finger in his chest. “You didn’t hurt me. You were nothing to me. A young girl’s fling. Nothing more.”

The knife twisted in his heart. “Prove it, then. If our past meant nothing, it shouldn’t bother you to have dinner with me tomorrow night.”

Natalie’s eyes went wide.

Eyes so big and blue, Lane could drown in them. “Well?”

Chapter 3

Natalie closed her eyes. If she said no to dinner, Lane would think she cared. That it bothered her to be near him. "Okay, I'll go."

Lane grinned. "The Cattleman's Steakhouse, say, five o'clock. I'll pick you up."

"Fine." She stood, stalked away from him and hurried to her car—trying not to let how he affected her show in each line of her rigid body.

She could still feel Lane's arms around her. His warmth and strength. She closed her eyes. He was the first and only man she'd ever loved. The first man she'd given herself to. Only to be tossed aside like yesterday's flavor of the day.

Why had she agreed to dinner with him tomorrow night? Because he'd caught her at a vulnerable moment? Again. Because she wanted to prove he didn't matter to her? But he did. He always had.

She had to get over it. But how?

An idea occurred to her. It was a shameful idea, she had to admit, but, oh, so tempting. She would seduce him. Knock him off his Christian pedestal and then dump him. Get him out of her system, once and for all, by breaking his heart, just like he'd broken hers.

She smiled and started the engine.

It was exactly like Mom's dollhouse Natalie and Caitlyn played with when they were little, a two story with a large pillared porch and a bay window. It was a haven from Lane and all the forgotten feelings he stirred in her.

Most high school graduates got a used car as a gift from their parents. Some got new cars. Natalie and her sister had gotten life-sized dollhouses that matched their parents' home, one on each side of their house.

At least there were some woods in between, so she had a little privacy. Daddy probably regretted that.

She unlocked the heavy door and slipped her boots off in the entryway.

"It's about time." Mama sat on the white couch in the formal living room.

So much for privacy. "Hi, Mama."

Her mother stood and greeted her with a warm hug. Her long, dark, former-Miss-Texas do was stiff with hairspray. "I'm so glad you're home."

What if she'd brought a cowboy home for the night and found Mama sitting on her couch? Of course, it would have been later, and Mama probably would have given up and gone home by then. Her insides churned, even though she hadn't brought anyone home in well over two years.

Her recklessness had embarrassed her parents, yet they'd loved and supported her. Until she got pregnant and lost Daddy. But Mama was still here, loving her.

"Sorry. I should have waited on the porch until you got

here, but I have a key, and I couldn't wait to hear about your first day. How'd it go at the Stockyards?"

"I'm organizing and giving the businesses advice this week. I've got two weeks to work up a proposal. I'll be ready by then."

"Good. I know you'll do great. You always have the cutest ideas." Mama sipped her sweet tea. "Did you see anyone you know?"

"A few people." She hugged herself. The subject of Lane was off-limits. "How long has Wyatt been married?"

"A few months."

"Why didn't you tell me?"

"You never want to talk about Hannah, so, I didn't mention it." Mama touched her arm. "Listen, sweetie. He's bringing Hannah over tomorrow night for a visit while he's gone to the rodeo. I thought you should know. We could talk to Wyatt. I hoped you might—"

"I already saw her." Twice. "Wyatt's wife came into Caitlyn's store while I was there today. She had Hannah."

"Oh, sweetie." Mama patted her arm. "You're missing out on so much. She's growing up so—"

"Wyatt won't let me near her. I don't want to talk about it." Especially not about the argument tonight.

"I think we could talk to him. When you're ready." Mama hugged her again. "If you want to come over for lunch tomorrow, Mary always has our meal ready at noon. Your father will be home and I thought it might be a good opportunity for y'all to talk."

Talk? When she hadn't seen Daddy since she'd told him she was pregnant? Since he'd blasted her for soiling the blueblood family name? "Thanks. But I've got a lot to do."

"Eventually, one of you will have to make the first move." Mama patted her arm and left.

The door shut. The house was too big. Too empty.

She was surrounded by luxury. By a mother and sister who still loved her, despite the things she'd done. Yet, she was still totally alone.

Natalie sank into the couch and drew her knees up until she was in a tight ball.

Lane raised his fist to knock, but the frosted-glass-paneled door swung open.

Natalie in red. Very little red. Cleavage and thigh with a scrap of dress in between. Bare, tanned, mile-long legs and stiletto heels to match the clingy dress. *Lord, what would happen if she sat down?* He couldn't take her anywhere in that.

Eyes, focus on her face. Red lipstick. Her hair a glossy, almost black curtain. Full lips that begged for his kiss. Curves that beckoned his arms. Absolutely gorgeous. And she'd be even prettier if the dress left more to the imagination. How could he get her to change?

He cleared his throat. "Are you ready?"

"Yes."

"You sure you'll be comfortable at the rodeo?"

"It's part of my job, and I'll have to get used to seeing Wyatt. Even though he's not the problem."

"In that?"

"What's wrong?" She struck a come-hither pose. "Does it offend your Christian sensibilities? Will you be embarrassed to be seen with me?"

He had to get her to change without insulting her, but he wouldn't get anywhere by preaching to her. "I'm afraid some guy might look at you wrong and I might bust him in the nose, which could get me fired. And besides, since you're working on publicity, don't you think you should dress a bit more professionally?"

She huffed out a sigh, rolled her eyes and disappeared down the hallway.

"Whew." The heaviness seeped out of his chest. *Lord, help.*

Every male head turned in their direction as Lane escorted Natalie around the arena. His fist tightened at his side. Yes, she'd changed into jeans and a hot-pink Western shirt. But her feminine allure was still firmly in place. Couldn't these guys see how she was hurting? How she only needed someone to really love her and introduce her to Jesus?

Lord, why did You have to make her so pretty? So soft? So curvy?

Her red fingernails rested on his biceps. Intoxicating perfume filled his senses. *Lord, help.*

"Not too close to Wyatt's box seats." She stopped.

"I'm sorry. I should have taken you to the other side of the arena."

"This is fine."

He glanced toward where Wyatt and Star had been last night. They were there with Lacie and her new husband, Quinn, along with another brunette.

The brunette waved. She looked familiar. "You know her?"

"Unfortunately."

The brunette stood.

"Great—I think she's coming over." Sarcasm tinged Natalie's tone.

"You don't like her."

"No. But you would. She's a Holy Roller, too."

He sighed. "Since she's a *Christian* lady, I bet she'd make a great friend for you. Give her a chance."

"Hey, Lane." The brunette stuck her hand toward him. "Kendra Wright. We met at church last week. Plus I saw you at Quinn and Lacie's wedding."

"Your husband is Stetson, the bullfighter." He clasped her hand. "He's a great guy."

"That's my guy." Kendra smiled. "Hey, Natalie, mind if I sit with you?"

"I'd love it." Natalie's smile smacked of fakeness.

"I better get my horse in gear." He turned to Natalie. "See you in a few."

She stepped close, her body firmly pressed against his. Her arms wound around his neck and she tipped her head back.

"Cut it out," he whispered, putting as much space between them as he could. "Is this about Wyatt?"

Her eyes went wide. "Of course."

"I thought he didn't matter."

"No, but it never hurts to make a guy jealous." Her lips beckoned. So soft and yielding.

Could he kiss her into loving him? Stupid. But he was almost willing to try. Especially with the reward of her kiss hanging in the balance. He'd surely drown. He had to win her heart for Jesus before he could win her heart for himself.

"Sorry, I can't help you out on that one." He unwound her arms from his neck and kissed the back of her hand. "See you after the rodeo."

The noodles he called legs still worked—by some miracle—and he strode toward the gate to saddle his horse. Natalie Wentworth still knocked him for a loop. Even after all these years.

Heart pounding like a jackhammer, he fumbled with the blanket and heaved the saddle on his horse's back. The big dun stood still and steady, swishing her black tail in anticipation while he tightened the girth around her sand-colored middle.

"I guess you and Natalie took up right where you left off in high school." Clay Warren's tone was taut.

Lane turned.

Clay's jaw tensed.

They'd been friends in school until Lane got into womanizing. Until that look of disapproval severed their friendship. "It's not like that."

"That was some hug."

"I ran into her here last night and asked her to dinner tonight." He adjusted his hat. "Remember, I'm a Christian now and I told her that. You should have seen the scrap of red dress she wanted to wear. I think she's trying to make Wyatt jealous."

"From where I sit, you didn't run."

He shrugged. "I figure I owed her. I used her once. She used me tonight." His heart squeezed.

"Are you sure that's all?"

Lane's gaze dropped to the dirt. "I love her."

"Lane Gray in love?" Clay's brows lifted. "With one woman?"

He nodded. "I think it happened back in high school. That's why I broke up with her. It scared me to death."

"You hurt her bad."

"Not according to her." Lane winced. "And then it seemed like she fell for you."

"She was just trying to make you jealous. And when I resisted, I became a game to her."

Just like tonight. She'd tried to use Clay all those years ago—to make Lane jealous. "She's been around the arena a few times?"

"You could put it that way."

"Because of what I did to her, you think?"

"You were a kid." Clay clapped him on the back. "And she made her own choices."

"Well, none of that matters. I love her."

"Kendra is a friend of Rayna's." Clay stroked the horse's jaw. "They've been praying for Natalie, but so far nothing's changed with her."

"I have to get through to her." A deep ache throbbed in his chest.

"Just don't let that scrap of a red dress get through to you." Clay grinned.

The mere thought of the red dress twisted his insides. "Pray for me."

Clay adjusted his cowboy hat. "Will do."

"What are you doing here, anyway? Didn't you retire a few years back?"

"I did. But I come once in a while to cheer the guys on."

"Where's Rayna?"

"She's terrified of bulls."

"Makes more sense than being afraid of dogs."

"Huh?" Clay frowned.

"Nothing. You know Rayna invited me to supper next weekend. Think she might invite Natalie, too?"

"I'm on it." Clay clapped him on the back again. "She's always said Natalie just needs Jesus and a good man."

He'd like to be that man.

Natalie rolled her eyes as Kendra took the seat beside her. "Why are you sitting with me?"

"I thought we might get to know each other better." Kendra smiled.

"Why? Aren't your friends over there?" Natalie glanced at Kendra's usual sidekicks—the ladies who avoided the Natalies of the world. Though Kendra's past aligned more with Natalie's, she'd never seemed interested in striking up a friendship before.

"To be honest, I'm not comfortable around Lacie's sister."

"Star is Lacie's sister? Why don't you like her?"

"No, I like her. She's very sweet. But since Wyatt and I have a history, I'm not sure she likes me."

Natalie elbowed her. "I guess we could start a club."

"Wyatt's exes." Kendra laughed.

"Something catchier than that."

"If we'd only dated, it would be one thing. But we weren't Christians then." Kendra hung her head. "And…I'm not sure how Star feels about our former relationship."

"Are they happy?"

"Very."

"I didn't know he married. Or that she adopted…" Natalie's voice cracked.

"She loves Hannah as if she were her own." Sincerity shone in Kendra's gaze.

Natalie's chin wobbled. "I'm glad. Really." She bit her lip, then rolled her eyes. "I guess she's a Christian, since Wyatt's on this Jesus kick."

"It's not a Jesus kick. It's a permanent change he's made, and, yes, Star is a Christian." Kendra laid a hand on her arm. "How do you feel about Hannah?"

Fire swept through her veins and she shook Kendra's hand off. "Did they send you over here to find out if I'm planning to cause them problems?"

"No. Nothing like that."

"Then why are you talking to me? You've never bothered before."

"And I'm sorry about that. When you were dating Wyatt, I decided to befriend you, but then you got pregnant and stopped coming to the rodeo. Still, I've prayed for you ever since."

Her mouth went dry. Why would this woman pray for her? She didn't need prayer. "Why did you want to befriend me?" Skepticism dripped from her tone.

"Because I've been where you are. I used to go from man to man, trying to fill the loneliness inside."

"You don't know anything about me," Natalie spat out.

"Maybe not. And I didn't mean to insult you. I only know

that I was lonely, no matter how many men there were. Until I finally found someone to fill the loneliness."

"Stetson? I don't think I could settle for one man. I'm having way too much fun." Her words rang hollow. Especially since she hadn't been with anyone since Wyatt.

"I love Stetson with everything I've got, but no—he didn't fill my loneliness by himself."

Natalie's insides bottomed out. "Your little girl?"

"No. It took Jesus to fill my loneliness. I couldn't settle with one man until Jesus settled me. And I couldn't be a mother until Jesus showed me how to love."

The big tractor in the center of the arena roared to life and the Chicago Bulls' theme song blared over the speakers.

Natalie huffed a sigh. Thank goodness she wouldn't have to hear any more Jesus talk for the night.

Lane parked his truck in front of her house, got out and came around to help her out. Her fingers clutched his arm. The drive was plenty well lit for him to get a final glimpse of her beauty. He focused on the house instead. He'd combated enough comments from the other cowboys about her to last him an eternity.

Besides, he didn't need to look. He'd memorized exactly how beautiful and tempting she was.

"Want to come in?"

Say no. Run. "Got any coffee?"

"This time of night?" Natalie frowned.

"I'm immune to it, doesn't keep me up."

"Okay." She let go of his arm and dug her keys from her purse.

The lock clicked open and he followed her inside. Fancy. Cream-colored walls, white furnishings and trim, shimmering gold drapery. Very formal. Not what he'd expect of Natalie.

"Come back here to the great room. It's not so stuffy. I

hate this room. Despite her horrible taste, my cousin Jenna is an interior decorator. I made the mistake of giving her free rein in here."

Now, that made sense. She led him to a room at the back of the house that had pale tan walls and deep brown furnishings, leopard paintings and fabrics, and throw pillows the color of the turquoise jewelry his grandmother used to collect. Now, this was Natalie.

"Make yourself comfortable." She slid off her boots. "I'll be right back with your coffee. I've got one of those fancy one-cup contraptions, so it's really fast."

He shouldn't have come in. This was a dangerous game. In her house. Alone. At night. With the woman he happened to love. A woman who didn't love Jesus.

He should leave. But he didn't want to.

A bookcase lined one wall. It was full of romance novels with scantily clad women in intense embraces with barechested men.

The painting over the fireplace caught his attention. Natalie's parents were in the middle, her dad in a suit, her mama in a black ball gown. Caitlyn, her sister, was on the right, clad in a bright blue gown, her hair a shade lighter than Natalie's and her eyes a darker blue. Pretty, but not as eye-popping as Natalie in hot-pink, form-fitting ruffles.

"Here it is." Natalie walked slowly into the room balancing a tray.

He hurried to take the tray from her.

"I didn't know if you like cream and sugar, so I brought the works."

"Black is fine."

"Ugh. So bitter." She handed the cup to him.

"Aren't you having any?"

"I'd never sleep a wink if I had a cup this time of night."

She looked him over. "But maybe lack of sleep wouldn't be such a bad thing if I had company."

His throat closed up. He sipped the steaming brew. "I'll be out of your way in a minute."

She shrugged. "Suit yourself. Have a seat."

If he sat in the chair, then she couldn't get too close. His traitorous feet headed for the couch, instead.

Natalie settled beside him, curling her long legs beside her, leaning toward him.

Drink the coffee and get out of here. He cleared his throat. "How's Caitlyn?"

"She owns clothing stores at the Stockyards and the Galleria. We're hoping she'll get the contract to clothe the Cowtown rodeo staff." She scooted closer to him. "How's the coffee?"

"Great."

"Good." Her fingertip traced his jaw. "I was hoping it wasn't too weak for you."

A tremor went through him.

"What are you doing?" He batted her hand away and edged away from her.

"Nothing." She slid closer.

His left hip lodged against the sofa arm.

She penned him in.

"Natalie, I'm not—"

She pressed a fingertip to his lips. "I just want to make sure you don't want to stay. We could have a lot of fun. For old times' sake."

Her white teeth bit into her full bottom lip. Tantalizing.

Lane's gaze jerked away from her and he jumped up. "I can't stay."

"I see." Hurt tinged her tone as she rose to her feet.

"I mean—I want to. I'd love to stay, more than you can imagine." He cupped her cheek. "But I won't."

He hurried toward the door.

* * *

Natalie charged after him. She couldn't let him ruin her plan. "What? Are you married or something?"

"No. But I'm a Christian." He turned to face her, gently taking her by the shoulders. "Listen to me, Natalie. You're beautiful. And I'd like to be your friend. You should be treasured. Not flaunted."

He sounded like her father. "Sounds boring."

"You're special. And I was too stupid to see how special back in high school. I took something I had no right to. And I'd like the chance to make it up to you. But if you try to seduce me, we can't be friends."

"Maybe I don't want to be friends." She moved in for the kill, sliding her hands up his muscled chest to curl around his neck.

He pulled free and sidestepped her. His hand gripped the doorknob. "I want you to go to church with me."

"Friends? Church?" She shook her head and stepped away from him. His words doused her flame more effectively than a cold shower.

"Please, Natalie. Value yourself." Sincere caring shone in his eyes. "If you don't, no one else will. Understand how special you are."

"Why are you being so nice to me?" Her voice quivered just like her insides.

"You deserve to be treated like a queen." Lane swallowed hard and cupped her cheek with a gentle palm.

Kindness transferred through his soft touch. No man had ever touched Natalie so tenderly.

Heaviness welled in her chest. Her insides twisted.

He was for real. Lane had changed. For the better, and she'd tried to ruin it for him.

She pushed his hand off the doorknob and opened the door. "You better go. You shouldn't be here."

His gaze settled on her lips.

Chapter 4

Natalie gave him a little shove, propelling him out the door.

"Sorry, my head says one thing, but I'm just a man." His gaze rose from her mouth to her eyes, his hand fell to his side. "Think about church."

She nodded, shut the door and leaned against it. No man had ever resisted her in full seduction mode. No man had ever turned her down.

She trudged to her bedroom, picked up the red dress from her canopy bed and shimmied into it. It fit perfectly. Her slender curves had survived Hannah and were still in all the right places. A flash of cleavage and expanse of thigh. What man wouldn't appreciate this dress?

A Christian man.

Cheap. She looked cheap. Like she'd sleep with anyone she met. And she had a few years ago.

But now, it was a false front. She'd slept alone since she

learned she was pregnant over two years ago. Except she didn't sleep, either.

She slipped the dress off, flung it across the room, and turned the shower on. Dirty. She felt dirty and her plan hadn't even worked. If Lane had fallen for her charms, would she have been able to go through with it? Probably not. Even though she still loved him. A tsunami brewed inside her.

Along with her unease about Lane, thoughts of Wyatt and Hannah churned to the surface. Along with this Jesus stuff.

The hot water soothed and she scrubbed her makeup off. She checked the hand mirror hanging on the shower wall to make sure she got it all. Dark circles sank in hollows under her eyes.

She turned the water off, dried and dressed in a jogging suit. Besides warding off the chill that wouldn't seem to go away, it provided good coverage for a change.

Maybe popcorn and a movie. Something to occupy her mind. She trudged back into the great room. The red light on her answering machine blinked on and off. She pressed the button.

"Hey, it's Rayna. Welcome back to town. Clay and I are having a dinner party next week and we wondered if you could come. Just a few friends like Kendra and Stetson. Nothing formal. Let me know if you can make it."

Now why would she want to hang out with Clay and Stetson and their wives? Two men who'd resisted Natalie's charms. Would Wyatt be there? Would Hannah?

No, surely not, or Rayna wouldn't invite her. But she did need to talk to Rayna and Kendra. She needed an experienced creative director and a photographer. Maybe she could convince them over dinner.

Lane knocked on the raw pine door of Clay's house. Imagine. Him and Clay Warren back on track. He needed all the

Christian influences he could get in his life. To keep him accountable. Especially with Natalie around.

It had been a long, slow week since their dinner. He'd almost called her a dozen times. Or turned into her drive.

The door swung open.

Natalie. Her blue eyes went wide. "I didn't know you were coming."

His smile froze. "Is that okay?"

"It's great." Her tone didn't hold any conviction.

"Great." Lane tried to breathe right. He hadn't told Clay to call off matchmaking efforts because he never dreamed she'd accept. Especially after their date, she wouldn't chance running into him. But maybe she'd wanted to.

Clay and Stetson sat in the living room mesmerized by a rodeo on the television.

"I don't think they even know you're here."

"Where are the women?"

"In the kitchen." She wore a dark gray pinstriped business suit with a lacy purple blouse underneath.

Full coverage, but still feminine. What was he thinking? She could wear a burlap sack and turn heads. Had she taken his advice to heart?

"You look beautiful."

"Thanks, but I think that's laying it on a bit. I was going for business casual since I got here early and just hired Kendra and Rayna to work with me on the Stockyards project."

So she'd come because of business. Not on the chance of seeing him.

"It's a massive undertaking. I have to get all of the businesses encompassed in the Stockyards in top shape before I can begin to publicize. Rayna used to be a creative director and Kendra was a photographer at an ad agency in Dallas, so they'll be definite assets."

The old self-sufficient, confident Natalie. Not the vulnerable, teary-eyed version. But both were hard-hearted toward him. And toward Jesus.

"Guess I should join the guys and let you get back to the ladies."

"I'm dying to return to the kitchen." She rolled her eyes.

Probably didn't feel comfortable with the other women.

"Lane." Rayna hurried toward him from the kitchen. "I'm so glad you could make it."

"Thanks for inviting me."

"Supper is on the table. I was just going to get the other men. Y'all go on in."

He mustered up a smile. "Great."

Great. An evening spent with a woman who didn't want to spend time with him.

Natalie scanned the gathering at the table. Besides her hosts, the group included Kendra and Stetson and Lane and her. Rayna and Kendra used to work together and would soon work with her. The men were bonded by rodeo.

Both other couples were married. With kids. Churchgoers. She stuck out like a mule in a room full of thoroughbreds.

Even with Lane. He'd changed. He fit in better with these couples than he did with her. What had Rayna been thinking, inviting them? Pairing them off?

The conversation went from rodeos and ranching to raising kids and church, to Kendra's early stages of pregnancy and morning sickness.

Natalie's stomach took a dive. She tried to focus on the decor. Cowboy culture mixed with modern pieces—a blend of Clay and Rayna.

"Awesome meal, Rayna." Lane set his napkin by his plate. "Since Rayna cooked and the ladies helped set the table, the guys should clean up."

"Aw man—" Clay winced "—you come here to show me up, Gray?"

"I like the way Lane thinks." Rayna elbowed her husband. "Come on, ladies."

The women filed out of the room.

Natalie lagged behind. Out of view of the men, she watched as the women headed toward the living room. She glanced toward the door and made a run for it.

If she snuck to her car and drove home, would that be so rude Rayna would back out of their deal? She'd have to go back in and play nice. But not now. She couldn't take another minute of happy-couple land, and she needed a breather or her face would crack from smiling.

She settled on the porch swing, swaying back and forth. The creak of the chain mingled with the bird chorus in the live oaks surrounding the house. She leaned her head against the chain.

The front door opened.

Lane?

Natalie straightened. Her hair snagged in a link and she tugged it free.

Kendra stepped out. "You okay?"

"Just enjoying the peace."

"Sorry for all the mom talk. I imagine you're uncomfortable."

With a lot more than that. "Why did Rayna invite me?"

"Because she's nice." Kendra settled on the swing beside her.

"And she wants to pair me off with Lane."

"I'll admit Rayna is known for matchmaking and she's pretty good at it. What's up with you and Lane, anyway?"

"We had a high school romance, back in the day."

"I'd say there's still a spark there."

"We're as mismatched now as we were back then. But on opposite ends of the spectrum now."

"Are you seeing someone?"

"Not at the moment." Natalie pushed off with her foot, setting the swing in motion. "Can I ask you something?"

"Sure."

"Back when you—before you met Stetson—did you ever hit a dry spell?"

"You mean—with men?"

"Yes."

"No. Looking back, I wish I had."

Natalie closed her eyes. "I haven't…"

"What?"

She shook her head. What was she thinking? She couldn't tell Kendra. They'd talked exactly twice now.

"I'm a great confidante. I figure if you want it told, you'll tell it—so I don't." Kendra made a zipper motion across her lips just as Natalie and Caitlyn used to when they were kids. But Kendra locked the zipper and threw the imaginary key over her shoulder.

Natalie laughed.

"Really, I don't repeat things. Not even to Stetson. And I'd like to be your friend."

A deep breath. "I haven't been with anyone since Wyatt."

"Wow."

"When I found out I was pregnant, Wyatt and I had already ended it." Her pent-up thoughts tumbled out with a rush of relief. "But I hadn't been with anyone else. Then he talked me out of the abortion, the nausea hit and I got so fat nobody wanted me. After Hannah's birth, I was depressed, along with being fat and ugly."

"I doubt that. You don't look like you ever had a baby."

"I got back in shape a few months later and scouted the rodeos and bars. Several times, I took a cute cowboy to my apartment in Garland, but I couldn't go through with it." Natalie bit her lip. "This sounds crazy, but every time I've tried to drink or have sex since I got pregnant, I feel sick to my stomach."

Kendra smiled.

"You think this is funny?" Natalie jabbed a finger at her. "If you tell anybody about this—"

"I won't. I promise. It's just that this all happened about the time Rayna, her sister-in-law and I started earnestly praying for you. Maybe you're convicted."

All the fire seeped out of her. "Convicted?"

"Pricked by your own conscience. God doesn't want that lifestyle for you. And maybe, deep inside, you don't want it anymore, either."

"But I don't want to be alone."

"Trust me, you can have a different cowboy in your bed every night and still be alone. Maybe it's time for you to make a change, Natalie. Come to church with me tomorrow."

It was almost tempting.

Natalie stood. "Could you tell Rayna I appreciate her inviting me tonight? And I look forward to working with both of you. But I think I'll skip the rodeo tonight and go home."

"Sure. But think about what I said."

Oh, she would. Her brain would spin with it for hours. For another sleepless night.

Natalie went straight to her walk-in closet. Did she have anything suitable for church? Why was she even considering going?

The red dress she'd worn to tempt Lane mocked her. She tugged it off the hanger. The black dress she'd worn to the bar in Denton and almost picked up the nameless cowboy was next. She flung both dresses on the bed, then jerked several scanty blouses and dresses from their hangers. Expensive clothes. Maybe she'd donate them to Goodwill.

No. No one should wear these. Except a hooker. For most of her adult life, she'd paraded around looking like a hooker. On purpose. No wonder the quality of men in her life had been so low.

Natalie dumped the dresses in the trash, sank to the bed and covered her face with both hands. *What is wrong with me? Help me.*

Who was she talking to? God? Was He listening?

"Okay, I'll go to church."

She tugged her pajamas on and sprawled across her leopard-print comforter. For the first time in years, her mind was at ease. Cottony, floating, at peace.

Lane stepped inside the deserted church lobby.

Deserted except for a woman who looked like Natalie from behind.

He did a double take. His steps stalled.

The soft dark hair, the curves were familiar. But the dress was all wrong. Turquoise. Short sleeves. Barely below the knee. Proper. Nothing Natalie would wear, though she'd shocked him with her business suit last night. But she wouldn't just show up at church. And her carriage was all wrong. No confidence. This woman fidgeted, shifting her slight weight from one foot to the other.

She turned as he approached. It was Natalie.

His steps stalled again.

"Hi." A shy smile.

Shy?

His tongue stuck to the roof of his mouth. "Hi."

"Aren't you going to say something cheesy, like how glad you are that I came?"

"I am. Totally glad. You look beautiful."

"Where is everyone?"

"Probably the fellowship hall. We gather there for coffee before class."

"Oh."

"Want some?"

"I could use a cup for courage. But I'd be uncomfortable with a bunch of people I don't know."

"You don't need courage. I think you know a lot of them. Clay, Rayna, Stetson and Kendra all attend here."

She looked like she might get sick.

"You okay?"

"I only went to church for a few years when I was a teenager. Not since then and never to this one."

"Well, I haven't been here long, so I can't promise you anything. From what I've seen, you might get a few hugs, but nobody bites."

She shifted her weight again.

"Ease up. Relax. Everybody's nice."

"They might worry the roof will cave in when they see me."

"I don't think so. They'll love you, if you let them. That's what Christians do."

"Don't you want to know what made me decide to come?"

"That's your business. I'm just glad you did."

She shrugged. "I'm so confused. I was hoping I could talk to the pastor. Wyatt tried to get me to meet with him a few years ago. Said he was easy to talk to."

"I'm sure he'll be happy to talk to you, during Sunday school or after services. And after that, I'd love to take you to lunch."

She smiled. "I'd like that."

The windowed door leading to the fellowship hall and classrooms opened. Kendra burst through, followed by Lacie.

Kendra hugged Natalie. "I thought that was you. I'm so glad you're here."

"Thanks." A hesitant smile.

"And Lane, you came back." Kendra gestured to Lacie and Quinn. "You know Lacie Gentry. Oops, I mean Lacie Remington."

A knot formed in Lane's throat.

"Of course." Lacie smiled. "We invited him to our wedding. Lane was the pickup man the night Mel—"

He swallowed the knot. "I always wondered if I could have…"

She patted his arm. "You did all you could. I was there. And Mel thought the world of you."

At least she'd managed to move on. Quinn was a good man. "Congrats again on your new marriage. How's your son?"

"Just left him in the nursery." She smiled. "Well-adjusted and happy."

"I'm glad."

"Um, sorry to interrupt, but could I speak with Lacie and Kendra alone?" Natalie's voice shook.

"Sure." Lane deflated. Why couldn't she talk to him? "Ladies, could you make sure Brother Timothy knows Nat would like to speak to him? And Nat, don't forget about lunch."

"I won't."

He headed for the fellowship hall. Alone. Did she care two hoots about him or not? At least she didn't complain when he called her Nat. And she'd agreed to lunch. Surely that meant something.

Natalie wrung her hands. "Do Wyatt and Star still attend here?"

"Yes." Lacie looked at the door she and Kendra had come through. "They should be along any minute."

"With Hannah?"

Kendra blinked, as if she'd just now thought of that complication. "She'll probably be in the nursery."

"I should leave." Natalie's eyes stung. "I don't want to cause them any problems."

"Star wanted to talk to you about Hannah." Lacie laid a hand on her arm. "Wyatt's all worried you might try to take her away, but maybe y'all can have a civilized conversation about it sometime."

"To be honest—" Natalie swallowed hard "—I'm not sure what I want. Concerning Hannah. I just know that I haven't been the same since Wyatt talked me into having her."

"You're a mama." Lacie gave her arm a gentle squeeze. "That changes everything."

"Don't leave." Kendra glanced down the hall. "Let me show you to Brother Timothy's office. Maybe you can talk to him during Sunday school. Lacie can prepare Wyatt for seeing you here."

"Great idea." Lacie nodded. "I'm on it."

Kendra linked arms with Natalie, led her to a door at the end of the lobby and knocked.

"Come in."

Kendra opened the door to reveal a man in his late forties or early fifties sitting at a desk.

The nameplate read Brother Timothy Andrews. Natalie had expected an older man. Didn't preachers have to be at least seventy?

"This is Natalie Wentworth. She wanted to speak with you."

"Natalie." He smiled. "It's so nice to see you."

She scanned his features. The youth director her father had tried to inflict on her. "Brother Timmy?"

"You two know each other?" Kendra frowned.

"He was the youth director at my parents' church."

"Wait—you grew up in church?" Surprise echoed in Kendra's tone.

"Just during my teen years. My sister loved the youth

group." *But I never got involved, no matter how hard Daddy pushed.*

"How is Caitlyn?"

"She's good. She owns two clothing stores."

"Which ones? Maybe my wife and I will check them out."

An image of him in cowboy gear brought a smile to her lips. "I can't picture you in cowboy-style clothing, but here's her card." She dug the card out of her purse. "When did you become Brother Timothy?"

"Actually, I'd always gone by Timothy, but during the years I worked with the youth, I did anything I could think of to try and connect with them." He shrugged. "Timmy sounded younger, less stuffy—so I went with it."

"I didn't know you used to be a youth director." Kendra turned to Natalie. "So this will be like talking to an old friend."

Not necessarily a friend. Brother Timmy had stopped by their house countless times—probably at her father's request—but she'd barely acknowledged him. Yet Daddy had probably filled him in on the errors of her teenage angst back then.

"I don't want to bother you. If you need to meditate or whatever you do before church."

His smile was kind. "I'm all prayed up."

Kendra cleared her throat. "Do you want me to stay?"

If anyone could understand her life, it was Kendra. Maybe having an ally would make this easier. A few weeks ago, she'd have laughed if anyone had told her she'd ever think of Kendra as an ally. More like a rival. At least, a few years ago, anyway.

"Would you?"

"Sure." Kendra shut the door.

He gestured to a chair. "Have a seat. I can assure you that whatever we speak of will go no further."

Natalie perched on the chair across from Brother Timothy's desk.

"What can I help you with?"

"Eighteen months ago, I had a baby. Out of wedlock." Her eyes stung.

Brother Timothy's expression didn't change. It held no judgment, just concern, as he handed her a box of tissues.

"I gave her up." Natalie pulled a tissue out and dabbed her eyes. "But sometimes, I think I hear her cry, and I dream about her all the time."

What was she doing here? Figuratively on the therapist's couch, where she never dreamed she'd end up. At least she sat in a chair and wasn't actually on a couch.

Brother Timothy leaned forward. "She was adopted?"

"Her biological father has custody."

"Do you trust your daughter's father to care for her?" His tone comforted her.

Natalie relaxed a little. "I don't know. At one time he was as unstable as me."

"What do you mean by unstable?"

"Relationships." Natalie pleated a fold in the fabric of her skirt. "Lots of them. For both of us. And we both used to drink pretty heavily."

"But you've both changed?"

Natalie rolled her eyes. "He supposedly became a Christian. He begged me not to abort her and let him raise her. At the time, I just wanted out."

"He is a Christian." Kendra clamped her lips shut. "Sorry to interrupt, but he's a member of this church and he's completely turned his life around."

"I see." Brother Timothy steepled his hands as if in prayer. "Did you see your daughter when you were in the hospital?"

"No. My mom tried to get me to, but I refused. I didn't care." *Or I didn't think I did.*

"But you do now?"

Natalie stood and paced the office. "I left Aubrey to live in Garland after I had her, but I'm the publicist for the Fort Worth Stockyards now. I've moved back to Aubrey and I'll have to work in the area for a while until I can get things organized enough to handle my work online." Her heels clicked across the hardwood flooring. "I've already accidentally run into her once and had a couple of tense run-ins with her father since we live and work in the same geographic area now."

"Did you think about her when you were in Garland?"

"My daughter has haunted me since her birth. But now it's worse. I can't sleep. I'm fidgety. I don't enjoy life like I used to." Men weren't a challenge anymore. And no comfort. "I need peace."

"And you thought talking it out might help?"

"Yes."

"But there's more, isn't there, Natalie?"

"What do you mean?"

Brother Timothy smiled. "Are you a Christian?"

"No." Sarcasm filled her tone. "If I were, do you think I'd have gotten pregnant outside of marriage, considered an abortion and given my daughter away?"

"It happens." He sighed. "More than you realize. Christians aren't perfect. We're just forgiven."

All the ones she knew sure seemed perfect. Natalie hugged herself. Forgiven sounded good.

"I'm living proof of that." Kendra's hand touched her shoulder.

She sank into the chair and the tears came again. "I miss her so bad. I didn't think I cared. I didn't want to care, but I do," she squeaked.

"I think you need two things, Natalie." Brother Timothy pressed a fresh tissue into her hand.

"What?" Natalie swabbed her face.

"We both know Aubrey isn't a whole lot closer to Fort Worth than Garland."

"True, but I have a house in Aubrey, my family is here and the commute is better."

"True, but I think the real reason you came home is your need to see your daughter. Perhaps only a few times to see that she's properly taken care of and to gain closure." Brother Timothy leaned back in his chair. "If that doesn't work, perhaps visitation. But I'm guessing you don't want to disrupt her life unless you find she's not well cared for."

A bubble of fear shot through her. What did she know about babies?

"I can assure you both—she's well taken care of." Kendra settled in the chair beside Natalie.

Natalie bit her lip. "What's the other thing?"

The pastor leaned forward again. "You need Jesus."

Chapter 5

Natalie attempted to laugh. But it sounded nervous. "You sound like my parents and sister. But even if I did need Him, He'd never take me on."

"Jesus takes on anyone who asks." Brother Timothy flipped his Bible open. "Let me share some scripture with you. Would that be all right?"

"I guess." Natalie shrugged. "But I'm not sure I can come to church here."

"You don't feel comfortable because your daughter's father is here?"

"I don't want to take her away. Not unless they're neglecting her."

"Wyatt and Star love her, Natalie. I promise." Kendra covered her mouth with her hand. "Oops. But it's true, they live for her."

Warmth crept up Natalie's neck. No telling what Wyatt had

said about her. What must the pastor think of her? Her gaze lifted to meet Brother Timothy's. "Did you know?"

"I figured it out." He nodded. "It's a small church. But I agree with Kendra, Wyatt and Star love Hannah. They're very happy."

"Then I won't disrupt Hannah's life. But I..."

"I suggest a meeting with Wyatt and Star here in my office. Perhaps visitation?"

"I'm not sure if I can even have that. Legally."

Brother Timothy looked thoughtful, but not judgmental. "If you like, I can talk with Wyatt first. Then perhaps we can set up a meeting and I could act as mediator."

The pressure in her chest dissolved. "That would be great."

A buzzer sounded.

"Is my time up?"

"That means it's time to gather for devotion and then go to class. But I don't have to be there."

"I don't think I should stay for the service."

"You can stay here in my office, if you like. I can turn the monitor on, so you can see and hear the service."

"Perfect." Kendra turned her chair to face the monitor. "I'll stay here with you, if you want."

A friend. Her first female friend, other than her sister and her cousin. "That sounds great." And to think at one time, she and Kendra had squared off over Clay at a rodeo.

"Let me show you that scripture." Brother Timothy turned the Bible so she could see.

But did she want to see? The pressure in her chest came back with full force. "I know all about it."

"You do?" Brother Timothy's gaze never left hers.

She looked down. "I may not have participated in church, but I heard a few things. I know Jesus died on the cross—supposedly for my sins. I know He rose again and I'm supposed to confess my sins to Him. Then I'm supposed to clean up my life and ask Him to be my savior. He's supposed to save my soul and get me to heaven."

"All true. Except, there's no supposedly about it and you don't have to clean a thing. Jesus will do that for you. He takes our filthy rags and washes us white as snow. You've got the head knowledge, you just need the heart knowledge."

She met his gaze again. "I've always wondered..."

"Yes?"

"Did He really mean me?" The things she'd done—how could Jesus accept her?

"He meant everyone. All you have to do is ask, Natalie. If you'll accept Jesus, He'll accept you."

Lane scanned the sanctuary as the church service began. No Natalie.

She'd left without him. Had she gotten cold feet? Changed her mind about him? About God?

"Expecting someone?" Stetson whispered.

"A friend. She was here earlier."

"Relax. Kendra texted me. She's in the office, watching on the monitor with Natalie."

"Why don't they join us?"

"Natalie didn't want to upset Wyatt and Star."

"What's up with Natalie and Wyatt?"

"I thought you knew." Stetson shook his head. "I'm not going there. That's Natalie's department."

The pianist began playing. Lane didn't bother with a hymnbook, he knew them all by heart.

The church had been redecorated since he was a kid. The old red pews and carpet had been replaced by more contemporary navy blue. But the piano was still there, probably the same one, and the hymnbooks transcended time. How had he stayed out of church so long? How had he never gotten it as a kid?

And now Natalie was here.

The third hymn faded away and Brother Timothy approached the pulpit, bowed his head and prayed.

If she became a Christian, they could start all over. With pure hearts. Free to love each other. If only Jesus could win her heart.

He tried to concentrate on the sermon. Brother Timothy always held his attention, but not today. He could only think about Natalie. And what was up with her and Wyatt?

The music began again. The altar call. Lane had pondered right through the sermon. Several people visited the altar. Lane joined them there.

Focus. He knelt there until his soul quieted, then returned to his seat.

The music ended and Brother Timothy closed the service in prayer.

The crowd filtered toward the lobby. He caught a glimpse of Kendra waiting there, but no Natalie.

She'd left without him. Even after he'd asked her to stay for lunch.

He neared Brother Timothy, anxious to ask how it had gone with Natalie and where she'd gone.

"She's waiting in your truck," Kendra whispered.

His grin spread straight through his heart. "Thanks." He bypassed the line shaking Brother Timothy's hand and headed for the door. It was rude. But he did it anyway.

He could see her through his tinted windows. In the middle instead of on the passenger's side. He jogged the rest of the way and pulled the door open. "Feel better about things?"

She nodded. "Can we get out of here?"

"Sure." His fingers itched to touch her hair. Her cheek. Her lips. But they had to start fresh. Without the physical stuff. He started the engine. "Where to for lunch? I think everyone pretty much goes to Moms on Main. Ever been there?"

"I love their food, but is that where Wyatt and Star go?"

"Probably." He followed the line of cars out of the parking lot.

"Then anywhere else."

"I know a great steak house."

"Yum."

"How did your talk with Brother Timothy go?"

"I think I'm a Christian."

Joy burst in his soul, despite her uncertainty. He pulled to the shoulder of the road and turned to face her. "You can't think you're a Christian. Doesn't work that way. You either are or you're not."

"It was weird—I knew Brother Timothy before. My parents dragged me to church during my teens and he was the youth director there." She lifted one shoulder. "At first I was uncomfortable, but he was very soothing. I don't understand it all. He read some scripture and I got this funny feeling in my chest."

"Did you say the sinner's prayer?"

"Yes."

"Did you mean it?"

Her eyes got watery and she nodded. "I'm a sinner and the only thing that will fix me is Jesus. But He's got a lot of fixing to do."

He got out of the truck, came around and opened her door. "Get out."

"Why?'

"Just humor me." He helped her down, then scooped her up and swung her around.

She clutched his shoulders. "What are you doing?"

"Celebrating! You're a Christian!" He set her down.

"Am I? I don't even know what it means. I've done so many horrible things."

"So have I. That means you're human. And I still struggle. You will, too."

"Struggle."

"Accepting Jesus as your Savior doesn't make life all rosy. Christians still struggle. With old ways. With life. With temptation."

"Like you did last week." Her cheeks pinked. "Sorry about that."

Natalie Wentworth blushed. He needed to mark his calendar. Jesus had done a miraculous work in her already.

"It's in the past and Jesus washed it away. Just like He washed away what I did to you in high school. He forgives and forgets. We're the ones who tend to hang on to past mistakes and still hold ourselves accountable." He picked her up again. "You're going to heaven when you die."

"You really think so?"

"I know so." And he was free to love her.

Natalie's stomach grumbled and she clutched a hand to it as Lane set her down again.

"Better get you some food." He helped her back into the truck and walked around it.

Settled in the driver's side, he glanced over at her. "I'd like to continue to see you, Nat. On a regular basis."

"I'd like that."

"But I need to know what the deal is with Wyatt." He started the engine.

Her gaze dropped to her lap.

"I'd like to start over with you, Natalie. Fresh. But we have to be honest with each other."

She huffed out a big breath. "Wyatt has a daughter, Hannah."

"And."

"I'm her mother."

His gut wrenched. Didn't see that coming. "Y'all were married?"

"No. I've never married anyone."

"He has custody?"

"Yes."

He waited for an explanation. But none came. Had she lost custody because she'd been promiscuous? No. That didn't matter. To the world or the courts. As long as they didn't move a child molester in, it seemed single parents could play musical bed partners as often as they wanted. And the court couldn't care less that the nuclear family had all but fallen by the wayside.

No. Mothers only lost custody if they were unfit. Drugs, usually. She was stronger than that and too smart. Maybe alcohol. She'd come from a bar the night she'd shown up at his door. Or maybe Wyatt had even more money than the Wentworths and he'd pulled strings to take Hannah away from her.

"Does he have a restraining order against you or something?"

"No. Nothing like that." Her voice grew soft. "But I don't want to disrupt her life. I just want to see her and I'm trying not to upset Wyatt so he'll let me. Brother Timothy wants to set up a meeting for us to talk it over."

"That's ridiculous. A mother shouldn't have to beg to see her daughter." No matter what she did.

"Does this change your opinion of me?"

"No. Whatever you did in the past, it's over, and you're different now. At least you didn't kill her."

He heard her sharp intake of breath. "Why would you say that?"

"Six months ago, my girlfriend got pregnant and aborted my baby. Without even telling me until it was over. Too late. That's what finally drove me to my knees and God."

He punched the steering wheel. "What kind of woman could even think about aborting a child?"

She didn't say anything and he glanced her way. All color had drained from her face.

"Sorry. Obviously, I still need to work on my anger. Not very appetizing lunch discussion."

"I think I'm just tired. I haven't slept well in forever. Until last night. Could you take me home?"

No. He wanted to spend time with her. "You need to eat."

"I'll eat a sandwich at home. I'm sorry."

"I was looking forward to lunch."

"Maybe another time."

Maybe? How had they gone from her waiting in his truck after church to 'maybe'?

"Hey, what did I do?"

"Nothing. I just need to get home."

To get away from him. Why? He'd told her it didn't matter to him. "What about your car?"

"I'll get Kendra to drive it home tonight. Hers and Stetson's place is down from mine."

"I could swing by and drive you to church tonight."

"Maybe."

Definitely the brush off. "Natalie, don't do that."

"What?"

He pulled into her drive and parked. "Push me away. I care about you."

She hugged herself. "I'm a mess right now."

"Me, too. Maybe we can clean up our messes together."

"I've been with so many…I think it's better if I'm alone for a while."

"Friends. That's all I'm asking." Okay, so it wasn't what he wanted, but it was a start. He held both palms up toward her. "Completely hands off."

"We'll see how it goes. But thanks."

"For?"

"Caring. Knowing everything you know about me and still wanting to be my friend."

"I'm no saint. I'm the one who…" He closed his eyes and shook his head. If only he'd realized what he had back then when he'd had her. If only he'd been a Christian and treated her right. "I've got my share of regrets."

She opened her truck door.

He reached for his own handle. "Let me walk you in."

"I'm fine."

Or rather, determined to be fine, even though she wasn't. She slid off the seat and slammed the door. Her shoulders drooped a bit as she hurried to her house.

Determined to be fine. Without him.

At least he didn't have to worry about her hanging out in bars and leaving with men she didn't know. *Thank You, Jesus.*

Friends? How could she be friends with Lane? Which was worse: having him near or not having him at all? A toss-up. It hurt either way.

She curled into her oversized sofa, a throw pillow pressed to her stomach.

Her phone rang and she grabbed the handset from the iron-and-glass coffee table.

"What are you trying to pull, Natalie?" Wyatt's angry tone chilled her.

Had he been this angry while speaking to the pastor? Or had Brother Timothy managed to soothe him, too?

At least until he'd heard her voice again. "I just want to talk to you. That's all."

"You're not taking her away from me. I'll take you to court."

"I don't want to take her away from you. I promise."

"Your promises never got me anywhere in the past."

She closed her eyes. "You're right. And I'm sorry. But I'm different now, Wyatt. I'm a Christian."

Stunned silence for several seconds. "I hope this isn't another one of your games."

"I'd never pretend to be a Christian. This is real."

"I never know with you."

"True—in the past. But you'll know—in the future."

"I hope so."

Had his tone softened a bit? "Are we meeting at the church sometime?"

"Yes." He hissed between clenched teeth. "Six-thirty on Tuesday night."

The line went dead.

She sank to the couch.

Her front door opened and Mama entered. Her smile held bigger wattage than pictures from her pageant days. "Durlene called me."

Clay's mom and Mama had been friends for years. Why was this news?

"Rayna said you were at church and she heard you spoke to Brother Timothy and got saved. Is it true?"

Natalie nodded.

"Oh, Nattie, I've prayed so hard for this day." Mama's eyes welled up. She settled next to Natalie and hugged her.

"Right now I don't feel very saved." Natalie hugged her mom tight.

"You'll have lots of days like that. I still have 'em and I got saved eleven years ago." Mama smoothed her hand down the length of Natalie's hair. "What's got you upset?"

"I had a fight with Wyatt on the phone."

"About Hannah?"

"I talked to Brother Timmy—I mean Brother Timothy—

about all these weird feelings I've been having about her. He thinks I need to see her."

"So do I."

"You've said that since the hospital." Natalie sighed. "Guess I should have listened."

"I know from experience, you can't become a mama and it not affect you. Wyatt doesn't want you to see her?"

"We're meeting with Brother Timothy tomorrow night about it."

"I think Brother Timothy took some counseling classes. He should be a great help."

"I hope so." Natalie's shoulders sagged. "Let's just say Wyatt's not thrilled. I think he's afraid I'll try and take her away from him."

"Is that your plan?"

"No." Natalie pushed away from Mama. She stood and paced, her heels clicking quick rhythmic steps across the tile flooring. "To be honest, part of me wants that. But I can't do that to her, and I have no rights. I gave her up. Even if I did have legal rights, I don't want to disrupt her life. I just want to be a part of her world. For her to know who I am."

"Wyatt will come around. Does he know you're a Christian now?"

"He thinks it's a trick." Natalie bit her lip. "I can't blame him. It's something I might have pulled a few months ago—if I'd thought about it."

"But that's not who you are now. I've seen God working on you for a while now." Mama cut her off midpace. "I'm proud of you."

Tears scalded Natalie's eyes. It had been so long since she'd made Mama proud. "Thanks. I'm sorry for all I put you through."

"It's in the past." Mama grabbed her hand. "Let's go tell your father."

Natalie's stomach twisted. She pulled her hand away. "He doesn't want to see me."

"He does. He's regretted what he said from the moment he said it. And you're a Christian now. That news might heal everything."

"Might?" Natalie lifted an eyebrow.

"There are no guarantees in life, Nattie." Mama held her hand out.

Natalie stared at it. Could Jesus heal her relationship with Daddy? She certainly couldn't do it on her own. She uttered a quick prayer and placed her hand in Mama's.

Mama tugged Natalie inside the house she'd grown up in. "Daniel! Daniel! You'll never guess who's here."

Natalie's insides quivered. Would her legs hold her up? She leaned against the Queen Anne table in the foyer. Her cousin's decorating touch was apparent in the creamy walls and matching satiny drapes.

"Daniel!"

"I'm coming, Claire. You'll wake the dead. What are you all fired up a—?" Daddy stepped into the entryway and caught sight of her. His eyes widened. A smile tugged at his mouth, but didn't quite form or rid his eyes of their sadness. "What are you doing here?" His tone was soft, regretful.

Regretful that she was here or that they'd slung angry words in the past? Natalie's stomach twisted.

"We have the most amazing news." Mama did a little bounce.

"Oh?" Daddy's features schooled into a mask, but he still couldn't hide all the pain and embarrassment she'd caused him.

"Natalie went to church this morning and she got saved."

Daddy cleared his throat. "Some weird cult?"

"No," Natalie said. "The same church Clay and Rayna go

to. I talked with the pastor, Brother Timmy—but now he's Timothy Andrews. He helped me realize I've lived a sinful life." Her voice quivered. "And I need a savior. I accepted Christ, Daddy."

His chin trembled.

Chapter 6

Daddy pulled her into an embrace. "Welcome home, sugar-plum."

Her tension melted away, leaving her weak and drained. "I'm sorry for—"

"No. I'm sorry. The family honor wasn't worth losing my daughter. I should have supported you."

Pressure built in her chest as if it would explode. A tremor moved through her and she tried not to sob.

Daddy hugged her tighter. "I've done plenty of shameful things in my life. Just never got caught. I never should have cast you to the wolves."

The front door opened and Caitlyn burst in. "What's going on that I had to drop everyth—?" Her sister's steps faltered. "Natalie?"

"Your sister's come home, Caitie." Mama's camera flashed. "It's perfect, having my two girls home, and now for eternity."

"Huh?" Caitlyn frowned.

"Nattie got saved this morning."

Caitlyn's frown turned upside down. "That's awesome." She joined in the hug.

Mama grabbed a tissue and dabbed carefully around her eye makeup. "It's everything I've prayed for. Except…oh, if only Millie were here."

Mama had pined for Millie—her missing sister—since her disappearance at sixteen. At least Natalie had managed to give Mama some peace.

Mama wiggled into the embrace.

A piece of Natalie's heart clicked into place. Now, if only she could sort through things with Hannah, and fill the hole Lane had left, maybe her heart would heal completely. Or maybe Jesus could fill the empty parts for her.

Natalie's hands shook. She crossed her legs, then uncrossed them.

Brother Timothy sat behind his oak desk. Star sat in the chair beside Natalie facing the pastor. Wyatt paced the office, like a tiger on display at the zoo.

Visine and concealer had erased all traces of her emotional reunion with Daddy over the last couple of days. Good as new.

New. A new creature. Brother Timothy had read her verses about Jesus making everything new. And Kendra had given her verses to read about God's view of sex outside of marriage. Why was she thinking of that?

She hadn't understood half of what the pastor told her. Except that God loved her. And He wanted her to change. To love Him. To honor Him with her life.

What was that verse about Him dwelling in her heart? What had Kendra said about once you become a Christian, Jesus went everywhere with you?

Be at this meeting with me, Jesus.

Numerous volumes lined the bookshelves, but the most important—the Bible—lay open on the pastor's desk.

Brother Timothy cleared his throat. "Well, since everyone's so talkative tonight, I'll start things off. Natalie just wants to see Hannah. Perhaps we could set up a visit."

"She gave up all her rights." Wyatt wheeled around toward the pastor. "I don't have to let her see Hannah."

"Think about what's best for Hannah. Natalie is her mother."

"It's too late for that. I have complete custody." He jabbed a finger at Natalie. "She signed the papers. This is all because she's jealous. I'm married and happy, and she can't stand it."

"That's not true." Natalie's eyes stung. "I'm happy for you."

Star stood and met Wyatt midpace. "Calm down. Give her a chance."

Why would Star give her a chance? Yes, Star really was that sweet. It wasn't an act.

"She had her chance." Wyatt growled. "She wanted to kill Hannah. The only reason she didn't is because I begged her not to, and then she couldn't get away from Hannah fast enough."

Natalie covered her ears. If only it weren't true. But it was.

Except the last part. She hadn't wanted to leave Hannah. She'd just thought if she did, she could get back to her carefree life. But it hadn't worked.

"One never knows the state of another's soul," Brother Timothy's voice soothed. "And I haven't known Natalie long, but I sense God doing a work in her."

"She's a player." Wyatt's jaw clenched. "You see what she wants you to see."

She flinched. He had her pegged all right. But something inside had ripped in two when she turned her back on Hannah.

Wyatt raked a hand through his sandy hair and turned

toward her, his hard features softening. "But I used to be a player, too. I reckon if I can change, you can, too."

She smiled. "I see you've changed. Guess I'm not the only one God's been working on."

He stared as if she'd sprouted a mane and tail. "I never imagined you in church, talking about God."

"Right back at you."

He grinned, but the smile soon faded. "I don't want Hannah getting attached to you and then you disappearing on her. You planning to stay in town? Being a part of her life?"

"To be honest—" Natalie swallowed hard "—I don't know. I just know that I haven't been the same since she was born."

"We don't have to tell her who Natalie is." Star settled in the chair beside Natalie again. "She can be a friend. If we downplay the whole thing, it won't be a big deal to Hannah."

An ally.

"You married a wise woman." Natalie nodded. "The right woman. I don't know how you got so lucky."

Wyatt laughed. "Me, neither. Reckon God smiled on me on that one." He stopped behind Star, his hands settling on his wife's shoulders. "Let me think on it."

"Fine." Natalie dropped her gaze to the hardwood floor. "It's a lot to take in."

"But—" he pointed at her again "—if you even think about trying to take her, I'll come after you with everything I've got."

"I'm glad you love her that much." Natalie's voice wobbled.

"Seems to me, having one more person to love her couldn't possibly hurt Hannah." Brother Timothy smiled. "I think we can work this out amicably."

"I'll be in touch." Wyatt offered his arm to Star and they left. Together.

Maybe she was a tiny bit envious of that kind of love. If Wyatt could find it, could she?

"That was certainly tense." Brother Timothy interrupted her thoughts. "You okay?"

"Yes. Thank you for refereeing. I hope the church pays you well if you deal with stuff like this on a daily basis."

Brother Timothy laughed. "That wasn't my first rodeo, but I think it went well. We made progress."

Natalie's insides warmed. "I really appreciate it. And I'm sorry I never gave you the time of day back when we initially met. Maybe if I had, my life would have turned out different."

"Perhaps." He nodded. "But you wouldn't be the person you are now, and there might not be a Hannah."

He was right. Something good had come from the mess she'd made. She stood, shook his hand and stepped out of the office.

Maybe everything would work out okay.

She turned the corner toward the exit. A large shape appeared just before she crashed into it. "Oh!"

A hard, muscled chest met her palms. Firm hands on her shoulders steadied her. A whiff of Irish Spring soap.

Lane.

Natalie jerked away from him.

"You okay?"

She nodded.

"I was hoping to talk to Brother Timothy. What are you doing here?"

"Wyatt and I met. About Hannah."

He searched her eyes. "How'd that go?"

"Better than I expected." Her voice cracked. "He's thinking about letting me see her."

"That's great." He hugged her.

A future with Lane could never be. She stiffened.

"Was it just me, or did we have a moment in my truck the other day?" His arms fell to his sides. "I thought we were growing closer."

"It was a nice moment. Let's leave it at that."

"Why?"

Because if you knew the truth, you'd hate me. "Because right now, I need to focus on Hannah and my job."

"I could help you with both. Emotional support."

"I appreciate it. But I have plenty of emotional support. My father and I reconciled our differences."

Lane's eyebrows rose. "I didn't know you'd had differences."

"Yeah. There's a lot you don't know about me." The bubble of hope in her stomach diffused. She sidestepped him. "Have a nice visit with Brother Timothy."

Maybe things could work out with Hannah, but not with Lane. If he knew the truth, he wouldn't have anything to do with her—especially after what had happened with his ex-girlfriend.

Lane could never be part of her future. She had to leave him in the past, where he belonged.

Lane wanted to go after her. The glass doors whooshed closed behind her and she bolted for her car. What was up with her? Was he a reminder of her old life? Did she not trust him? Maybe if he gave her space, she'd come around. It was the last thing he wanted. But if he pushed her, she might decide the last thing she wanted was him.

"Lane?" Brother Timothy called.

He spun toward the pastor. "I was hoping you had a minute to talk."

"Come on in."

"Were you leaving?"

"No. I have a counseling session in twenty minutes. Coffee run. Want a cup?"

"Sure." Lane fell in stride with the pastor down the long hallway toward the fellowship hall.

"What can I do for you?"

"I feel—" he groped for the right word "—unsettled." A weak word to describe the churning in his soul. But it was all he could come up with.

"You're moved into your house? Job's okay?"

Lane followed the pastor to the coffeepot. "Everything's great. I just feel like there's something God wants me to do. But He's not telling me what." He'd thought Natalie was his mission, but he'd failed there.

Brother Timothy poured two cups and handed Lane one. "Maybe teach a Sunday school class?"

Alarm shot through his chest. "I don't think I've been in the Bible long enough to teach anyone else about it."

"You'd be amazed what teaching a class can teach you. It forces you to study." Brother Timothy added cream and sugar, then took a sip and closed his eyes. "Mmm. Been needing this."

Lane sipped his steaming brew, strong and black. Perfect. "I don't think teaching's my calling."

"Maybe youth. Stetson could always use some volunteers. Especially since Kendra's battling morning sickness and doesn't always make it for class on Sunday."

Lane's heart warmed. Youth. Some of those teens didn't know any more about the Bible than he did. He could learn right along with them and be useful at the same time.

"Pray about it." Brother Timothy clapped him on the shoulder.

"I will."

"Anything else on your mind?"

Natalie. As usual. "I saw Natalie on the way in. Is she okay?"

"I think so."

"Do you think she'll attend church here?"

"Maybe. If not, maybe she'll attend with her parents. The

important thing is, she knows she needs church now." Brother Timothy set his coffee on one of the long tables, settled in a chair and motioned for Lane to do the same.

Lane sat. "I hurt her once. A long time ago. And I'm afraid my betrayal set her on a destructive path—one bad decision after another."

"She made her own decisions, and you can't change any of that."

Lane sighed. "Wish I could."

"All you can do is be kind to her now."

"I've tried, but she won't let me near enough."

"Just be her friend—even if it's from afar. Everyone needs a friend."

Friends with Natalie Wentworth? He'd offered her friendship. But actively pursuing it might kill him. Lane drained his coffee. "I'll let you get back to your office. Thanks for the ear and the advice."

"Any time." Brother Timothy shook his hand.

Lane headed for the exit. The shambles of his relationship with Natalie was his own doing. There was no one to blame but himself.

What had he thought—that she'd fall into his arms? She'd done that once and lived to regret it. And, apparently, she couldn't get past those regrets to see who he was now.

He'd just have to work harder to show her.

Lane entered the back lobby of the Cowtown Coliseum. Finally Friday. Still an hour before the rodeo. With his horse unloaded and saddled up, he'd have plenty of time for supper from the concession stand.

Natalie strolled several feet ahead of him, dressed conservatively in jeans, boots and a frilly Western shirt. And still turning heads as she went.

"Hey, gorgeous." A cowboy blocked her path. "Long time, no see. I hear you're the new publicist."

Lane's heartbeat stuttered. He knew this guy. One of the bronc riders. One who hit on every attractive female who crossed his radar.

"Yeah. I'm on my way to the office." She sidestepped the cowboy.

"How about a private party at my place?" He cut her off again. "A little beer. Maybe some dancing. See where it takes us?"

Her posture stiffened. "No, thanks."

"My pool will be open soon for the season. Remember that time we—"

Lane jogged up beside her. "Natalie."

She jumped. "What?"

"I've been looking for you everywhere."

"Why?"

"I missed you." He pulled her into his arms.

"Sorry, man, I didn't know you'd staked a claim." The cowboy sauntered off.

Lane's blood boiled. At the cowboy's attitude and Natalie's nearness.

Her palms pressed against his chest as she strained away from him. "What are you doing?"

"Letting these guys think you're my girl." And he certainly didn't mind the benefit of being this close to her.

"Why?"

"So you won't have to get hit on at every rodeo." He let go of her.

She was quick to put some space in between them. "I'll have to be more careful and make sure I clear out before the cowboys start arriving."

"You should be able to go wherever you want without worrying about anyone bothering you."

"In a perfect world, yes." Her gaze dropped. "But I've been less than perfect. I'm reaping the rodeo regrets I sowed."

"But you shouldn't have to. You could press sexual harassment charges against him."

"Yeah." She rolled her eyes. "Causing a scandal right off would endear me to everyone around here."

"Then I'll act as your bodyguard on rodeo nights."

"You don't have to do that. I'll be fine."

"I've seen your definition of fine." He glared at the departing bronc rider. "Besides, I want to help you."

"No."

He set his hands gently on her shoulders. "Let me do this for you."

"Why?"

"Because—I'm sorry. For treating you the way I did in high school."

"You've already told me that. It's okay."

"No, it's not. It will never be okay. And I'm sorry for the way every other jerk has treated you."

"None of that was your fault."

"Yes, it was. If I hadn't…maybe you wouldn't have…I'm sorry." How could he make her realize her value? He cupped her face in his hands.

She didn't stiffen or cringe at his touch.

"So beautiful." So hurt and used. He tipped her chin up and claimed her lips.

A tender caress. Innocent and sweet. But he'd be hard-pressed to keep it that way.

Chapter 7

Natalie melted into his kiss. It was gentle and soft, but reached to the depths of her soul. Her arms twined around his neck.

Lane pulled away long before she wanted him to.

Her lips trembled. "Didn't you say something about hands off?"

"Word travels fast around these parts. Now all these guys will think you're spoken for. They'll leave you alone."

Her heart turned over. He'd kissed her for show. Not because he'd wanted to. She couldn't let him see her disappointment. "Thanks."

He grinned. "I don't think I've ever been thanked for a kiss."

"I doubt you've ever kissed anyone just for show before."

"Natalie, I—"

"No. Really, I appreciate it. This way I won't have to fend off advances while I get used to my new skin. You've made everything easier for me." Except for the gaping hole in her heart. "But don't try to take advantage of the situation. That's the last kiss you get." She wagged a teasing finger at him and walked away, willing her knees not to cave.

Don't follow me. Don't follow me. Don't follow me.

He didn't. Why did that disappoint her?

Her breathing slowed as she put more distance between them. That kiss had turned her to heated mush. One minute she'd wanted to take him home for the night. The next, she could have killed him.

Were Christians supposed to have such thoughts? Had anything really changed inside her? Had anything really happened in Brother Timothy's office the day she got saved?

Natalie and Kendra walked through the empty church lobby toward Brother Timothy's office.

"He's probably working on tomorrow's sermon. Do you really think he's got time to talk to me again?"

"Of course." Kendra patted her arm. "Look, his office door is open."

Natalie knocked on the open door and peeked inside.

The pastor looked up from his desk. "Ah, Natalie. I'm glad you came back. For future reference, we have Sunday and Wednesday evening services, too. Not just Sunday morning." His teasing manner took the sting from his words.

"Yeah, I'm working on that. This Sunday, I'm going with my parents. In the meantime, do you have a minute?"

"Have a seat."

"Are you sure you want me to stay?" Kendra hesitated at the door.

"Yes, please." Natalie sank into the chair facing the pastor and waited until Kendra sat down next to her, then took a deep breath and gathered her thoughts. "Sometimes, I don't feel like a Christian."

Brother Timothy laughed. “I’m sorry. I know it’s not funny, but welcome to my world. I can’t tell you how often I don’t feel like a Christian.”

“But you’re the preacher.”

“Yes, but I’m still a man.” He propped his elbows on his desk, steepling his hands. “How do you feel when your thoughts or reactions aren’t Christian?”

She closed her eyes. “My insides churn.”

“That’s good. That’s Jesus convicting you. If you didn’t feel that, I’d worry about you. But since you do, that proves you’re saved.”

“But I felt that way, even before I prayed with you.”

“For how long?” Kendra asked.

“Over two years.”

Kendra’s hand went to her heart. “About the time Rayna, her sister-in-law, and I started praying for you.”

Natalie’s eyes misted. “Really. You think…?”

“I know.” Brother Timothy nodded. “There’s power in prayer.”

“Thank you.” Natalie blinked several times.

Kendra patted her arm. “Thank God.”

“Do you feel better about your salvation?” Brother Timothy asked. “That it’s real?”

Warmth flooded through her. A comforting presence. “Yes.”

“Good.” He pulled a Bible from the shelf beside his desk and handed it to her. “Take this. Once you finish the verses I gave you, I always suggest that new converts start reading John in the New Testament, then through to Revelation and start over in the Old Testament.”

“You already gave me a Bible the other day.”

“Now you’ll have two, one for home, one to keep in your car. Bring any questions you have my way. If I can’t answer them, I’ll study on it and let you know.”

"There are things you don't know? About God?"

"No one knows everything about God. Not until we get to heaven. One other piece of advice I can offer."

"What's that?"

"If there are people in your life who make you forget you're a Christian, avoid them."

Natalie swallowed hard.

Avoid Lane? With all of Cowtown thinking they were an item?

Natalie stood near her sister for moral support as the decision maker for the Stockyards Championship Rodeo surveyed Caitlyn's clothing store.

"You carry all the major brands." Dressed in a business suit, her blond hair pulled into a tight chignon, the woman looked anything but rodeo. She typed something into her iPad. "Your stock and displays are exactly what we're looking for. I think all of our rodeo personnel can find anything they might need right here in your store."

"And don't forget Caitlyn owns a second store in Dallas." Natalie handed her Caitlyn's business card. "Anything not in stock here can be pulled from there."

The woman looked up from her tablet. "I'm recommending you for the contract."

"Wonderful." Caitlyn remained professional, though Natalie knew fireworks burst within her, matching her own. "I'm so pleased you like the store."

"I can't make any promises, but the Cowtown management team usually trusts my judgment." The woman slid her iPad into her briefcase. "I'll be in touch—probably by the end of the week."

"Thank you."

The woman exited.

Caitlyn whooped and turned to face Natalie.

"I knew you could do it."

"I couldn't have." Caitlyn shook her head. "Not without you. You always give me just the right shove."

The sisters linked elbows and did a little square dance.

Yes, work could fill her empty spots inside. And if Wyatt would let her see Hannah, she might be okay. Who needed what's-his-name?

The bell rang above the door and their dance stopped.

What's-his-name strode in. "Hey, what's going on in here?"

"Lane? What are you doing here?" Caitlyn's wide eyes swept from Lane to Natalie.

"I moved back a few months ago. Didn't Nat tell you?" He set a large leather saddlebag on the counter.

"No."

His green gaze settled on Natalie.

Her insides squirmed. "Caitlyn's probably going to get the contract for Cowtown personnel clothing. We were celebrating."

"Congratulations." His eyes never left Natalie's. "Guess I'll be getting my working gear from here."

"You work at Cowtown?" Caitlyn's surprised tone promised a third degree later.

"He's a pickup man there." If he didn't stop looking at her like that, he might have to pick her up off the floor. "What are you doing here?"

"I saw your car out front." He opened the satchel. "I brought you something. Take a look."

Natalie leaned toward the counter without moving any closer to Lane.

He stuck both hands in the satchel and pulled out a ball of reddish-brown fur. "Sorry to wake you up, little one, but I want you to meet someone."

The puppy yawned and shook floppy ears. Feet too big for its body dangled over Lane's hand.

"Aww. Is he yours?" Natalie scooped the puppy out of his hands and cuddled it to her cheek.

"No, he's yours."

"What?"

"I rescued him from the shelter with you in mind."

"Why?"

"I thought he might get you past your fear of dogs."

"Good luck with that." Caitlyn chuckled. "He's a Lab, isn't he?"

Natalie stiffened. "He'll grow up to be huge."

"And you'll be there from the beginning. Labs are one of the most gentle dogs there are and very protective of their owners."

"This is a great idea, Nat." Caitlyn cooed at the puppy. "You can live in Garland without running into a loose dog, but not in Aubrey."

The puppy lathered Natalie's cheek with a sloppy kiss. Her frightened heart melted. She snuggled him close once more.

"I'll take that as a yes." Lane grinned.

"I'm never home during the day. He can't stay in my house."

"You've got that porch in the back." Caitlyn scratched the puppy's ear. "The rails are close together around the deck part. We could rig some kind of gate across the opening. And I bet Lane could find someone to build you a fenced-in area."

"Better yet, I'll build it myself." Lane folded his arms across his chest.

"What?" Natalie squeaked.

His bulging biceps strained at his sleeves. "You don't think I can? I've built a few fences in my life. Just place your order and I'll make it happen."

"You can't turn down an offer like that." Caitlyn—the traitor—obviously enjoyed watching her squirm. "Nat's always wanted a white rail fence."

"Done. I'll put in wiring at the bottom until this little guy gets too big to slip through."

"I'll pay you." Maybe that would hurry things along if he worked by the hour. How had she gotten sucked into this?

"No way."

"You can't buy me a dog and build a fence for free."

"I didn't buy the dog from a breeder or anything. I rescued him from the pound." He held her gaze. "And I figure I owe you. A lot more."

Pins pricked at the back of her eyes. She blinked. "I'll buy the supplies."

"Deal." He offered his hand. "On one condition."

She arched an eyebrow.

"I'm starting a fencing company. Can I put a sign up to advertise?"

"Sure." *Just get it over with. Fast.*

"You want it around your whole place?"

Yes. But that would keep him around longer. "The back will suffice." Forced to touch him, she clasped his hand. Electricity shot up her arm, and she jerked away. If only she could build a fence around her heart.

"I'll be there in the morning. Just show me where you want it."

It really was sweet of him. She should act more grateful. "It's very thoughtful of you—I mean the puppy. Well, and the fence. But especially the puppy."

"Thought he could help you and maybe fill some empty spots."

She blinked again. A puppy to keep her company while she waited to see her daughter. If she ever did.

"I bought some food and a doghouse to go with him. I'll put them in your car."

"What a guy." Caitlyn scanned from Natalie to Lane. "You think of everything."

"I'm just glad she accepted. I'm not sure how Barney would've liked me bringing a puppy home." He ran his fingers through the puppy's plush fur, grazing Natalie's hand again. "He needs a name."

Yes, he did. But she couldn't think past the fireworks shooting through her veins.

"You can't name a puppy quickly." Caitlyn scratched the puppy's ear again. "She'll have to get to know him and see what fits."

"I better get out of here. Want me to take him until you get off work?"

"No. This is my last stop for the day. If you'll load his gear in my car, I'll take him home. My car's unlocked."

"You really should lock it up. We're not in Aubrey anymore, Dorothy." Lane turned away. "See you in the morning."

The door shut behind him and Natalie started breathing again.

"He loves you." Caitlyn's sigh came out all mushy.

"What?"

"Why else would he get you a dog and build you a fence?"

"He got me the puppy because he feels guilty for using me and dumping me in high school. The fence is to advertise his new business."

"I don't think so. I think your long-ago high school romance stuck with him. What about you? Did it stick with you?"

"No." Her voice cracked. Drat.

Caitlyn propped her hands on her hips. "Who are you trying to convince? Me or yourself? Sometimes you never get over your high school sweetheart." Caitlyn's gaze glazed over.

Natalie knew exactly who was on her mind. "Do you ever think of Mitch?"

Caitlyn paled. "No."

"You sure about that?"

"Positive." Caitlyn reached for the puppy. "So what are you going to name this little guy?"

Her sister's quick subject change spoke volumes. She wouldn't mention running into Mitch—for now. Or that he'd asked about Caitlyn. Not yet. Obviously he'd never forgotten Caitlyn. And though she wouldn't admit it, Caitlyn wasn't over him.

Natalie was trapped in the same high school time warp as her sister. She'd never gotten over Lane either.

Lane stepped up to the porch and knocked on the door. Rapid-fire puppy barks answered.

"Hush now," Natalie's stern tone came through the wood. The door swung open.

Natalie, in Western gear and bare feet, snuggled the puppy close.

"You didn't even ask who it was."

"I checked the peephole. Relax, we're back in Aubrey, Toto."

Not a speck of makeup adorned her face. Beautiful. Even with tired, bleary-looking eyes.

His heart stammered with memories of the last time he'd been here.

But she was different now. And he'd accepted Christ months ago. So why did he want to pick her up and carry her to her bedroom? Why did past pleasures have to haunt him?

Past sins. Sins he'd inflicted on her innocence.

"He kept me awake most of the night, whining on the back porch. I gave in and brought him in and he still wouldn't hush. I finally had to let him in my bed so I could sleep."

Why'd you have to mention your bed? He cleared his throat. "I should have warned you. He misses his mama."

"So much for not letting him in the house." She rolled her eyes. "You're early."

"I wanted to find out where you want the fence before you leave for work."

"Here." She handed him the puppy. "Take him out before he has an accident. I'll get some shoes on and be out in a minute."

The door closed in his face.

He held the puppy up, eye to eye. "She's fallen for you but obviously not for me. Can you help me out here?"

The pup whimpered and Lane set him down in the wildflower-spattered grass by the porch.

The door opened, and Natalie strode out. She scanned the trailer on his truck, piled high with fencing. "Isn't that too much stuff?"

"I'd rather have too much than too little. I hope you don't mind vinyl instead of wood. No rot and no paint."

"Sounds perfect. You've been to the building supply already?"

"No. I had this in my shop for my fence. But I don't know when I'll get it started, so might as well use it."

"Come around back."

He followed, glad to follow her anywhere. In the backyard, he focused on the porch surrounded by a deck.

"I'm thinking a twenty-by-twenty enclosure straight out from the house about here." She walked the imaginary line. "Around the porch and deck and back to the other side."

He scanned the yard. A barbed-wire fence ran across the back about thirty feet away from the house. "I could fence in your whole place."

"Forty acres?"

"Sure."

"It's already fenced and there's no need to have a fancy new fence on all of it. Just the enclosure for the puppy will be fine."

"If I build a fence back here, no one will be able to see it for advertisement."

"True." She tapped her chin with her index finger.

"I could take the barbed wire down and rebuild with vinyl, then go ten feet or so out from each side of the house and up the sides, to where the back and sides would all be enclosed." He pointed to the puppy. "This little guy will need some space when he grows up."

Natalie nibbled her lip. "Oh, all right. But not all the way to the barbed wire and don't take it down. Daddy has longhorns in the pasture part of the time." She checked her watch. "I've got to get ready for work."

Music began playing: "There's Gonna Be a Heartache Tonight." Natalie dug in her pocket and pulled out her cell. She frowned at the screen and pressed a button.

"Hey, Wyatt, what's going on?"

Lane's heart stilled.

"Oh." Her eyes lit up. "That's wonderful. Of course I'll be there. Oh, Wyatt, thank you so, so much." She paused and turned her back to Lane. "I will. I'll be on my best behavior."

A tremor moved through her as she ended the call and stuffed thc phone back in her pocket.

Lane set his hands gently on her shoulders and turned her to face him. "You get to see her."

Her chin trembled.

"Steady. You'll do fine." He pulled her into his arms.

She inhaled a shaky breath, her face pressed into his shoulder. "I'm not sure. What if I cry? What if I get all emotional and scare her? What if I don't feel anything? What if I'm a horrible mother?"

"When do you see her?"

"Saturday."

"It's only Tuesday. You've got all week to settle down—to prepare yourself. You're already feeling something, which means you're not a terrible mother."

"You have no idea." She nodded against him, sucked in a

deep breath and pushed away from him. "But I have to pull it together. For her sake."

Yep. A definite heartache tonight. His.

She swiped her hand across her eyes. Her ringtone started up again. Her eyes went huge. "What if he changed his mind?"

He settled his hands on her shoulders again. "I doubt it. See who it is."

Natalie dug the phone out again. A relieved sigh. "It's Caitlyn." She blew out a big breath and answered.

"Why are you calling so early?" She paused. "Of course I'm up, but it's really early for you to be up and lucid enough to call." Her eyes lit up again. "That's awesome! I knew it. I just knew it." She pressed a hand to her heart. "Yes. Definite cause for supper. I have news, too. I'll meet you at Moms on Main around six."

She hung up and slid the phone back into her pocket.

"More good news?"

"The best. Caitlyn officially got the clothing contract for Cowtown."

"That's wonderful." He opened his arms. "Celebratory hug?"

Natalie cleared her throat and punched him in the shoulder. "I better finish getting ready for work. Where's Rusty?"

Another man? Lane's heart crashed. "Rusty who?"

"The puppy." Her voice went up an octave as her gaze searched the yard. "Rusty, here boy."

His chest filled with air again. Lane caught a glimpse of the puppy behind a bush. "There he is. He's fine."

She propped her hands on her hips. "Can I trust you to babysit him or should I pen him up on the back deck?"

"He better get penned up since I'll be concentrating on the fence. Go on and get ready. I'll take care of him."

Her gaze narrowed. "I don't want him getting in the road. I know it's a ways from the house, but he might wander."

Lane scooped Rusty up. “Don’t worry. I’m penning him up right now.”

She turned and headed back to the house.

His arms had felt so good around her. So right.

But Natalie didn’t even trust him with her puppy. How could he ever get her to trust him with her heart?

Natalie speared an avocado slice from her California salad at Moms on Main and popped it into her mouth. Smooth and creamy. The food always drew a crowd. People streamed in even on a Tuesday evening.

“Thanks for helping me get the contract.” Caitlyn sipped her tea.

“Your store had the goods. It just needed a little streamlining.”

“I almost feel like I had an unfair advantage with my publicist-marketing-major sister.”

“I worked with the other stores as closely as I did yours, but your store was the only one that already carried all the rodeo gear required. So you’re a pretty good marketer yourself.”

“You’ve taught me so well, I’m beginning to see that every business needs its own special touch.” Caitlyn gestured to their surroundings.

Natalie scanned the antiques lining the walls and shelves of Moms—everything from baby carriages to antique phones. An ambiance all its own. Just what every business needed.

“So what’s your news?”

Natalie swallowed hard. “Wyatt’s letting me see Hannah.”

Caitlyn grabbed Natalie’s hand. “That’s awesome! When?”

“Saturday. Quinn and Lacie are having some friends over for a trail ride. I’m supposed to be casual.” Natalie’s hand shook beneath Caitlyn’s.

“Casual? Meaning?”

“Meaning—I don’t tell her who I am. I’m just a friend

along for the trail ride. I don't grab her up and hug her." Or blubber over her.

A worried frown creased Caitlyn's forehead. "Can you do that?"

"I have to if I want to see her. Wyatt wants to take it slow."

"But not tell her who you are?"

"Not yet. It was Star's idea. That way it won't be a big, jarring deal for her. Once I see her, spend time with her—it might be enough for me. I'm not sure I want or deserve a place in her life. She already has two parents." Natalie's voice cracked. "She doesn't need me."

"Every little girl needs her mother." Caitlyn nibbled her lip. "So what if you want more?"

"We'll see."

Caitlyn squeezed her hand. "I'm proud of you."

"For what? Giving up my daughter?"

"Stop dissing yourself, Nat. It was the right thing for you to give Hannah up. It was best for her at the time. But since then, you've made a major turnaround. You're a Christian now." Caitlyn leaned toward her. "You may not realize it, but you're like a different person. It's as if the last ten years or so never happened. I got my sister back. And I really missed her."

"Me, too." Natalie sighed. "Sorry I dropped out on you. And thanks for never giving up on me."

Caitlyn squeezed her hand again. "We better get busy on these salads."

"I'm not in any hurry to get home."

"Don't you need to check on your puppy?"

"I named him Rusty. But he's not alone. Lane is there."

"You think he's still working on the fence?"

"I don't know. But I don't want to find out. I was thinking about hanging out somewhere else until it gets dark, just to make sure."

"Why do you want to avoid him?"

Lots of reasons. "Brother Timothy said to avoid people who make me forget I'm a Christian."

"Do tell. How does Lane make you forget?"

"He kissed me." Natalie forked a large bite of salad into her mouth so she'd have no room to elaborate until she gauged Caitlyn's reaction.

Caitlyn smirked. "When?"

"Before the rodeo Saturday night." She rolled her eyes. "And I had decidedly un-Christian thoughts. But don't get any ideas." *He only did it because I ran into this bronc rider I used to—* "This guy made a pass at me and Lane came to my rescue. He kissed me to convince the other cowboys we're dating, so they'd leave me alone."

"You sure that's all there was to it?"

"Positive." A knife twisted in her heart. "He pretty much told me so."

"Maybe that's what he wants you to think because he's not sure how you feel about him."

Natalie pressed her hands to her temples. "I don't need any confusion right now. Or anyone who makes me think decidedly un-Christian thoughts. I've got enough of both without Lane Gray in my life."

Caitlyn's gaze cut toward the door. "Speaking of your walking temptation."

"No."

"Yes. And he's coming this way."

Chapter 8

"Ladies." Lane tipped his hat and noticed the tightening of Natalie's mouth when she saw him.

"Hey, Lane." Caitlyn smiled. "Place your order and join us."

"I wouldn't want to interrupt the celebrating."

"You won't. You can help the celebrating. And Nat owes you a meal for that fence."

"If you're sure?"

Natalie looked anything but sure. But he couldn't pass up the chance to spend time with her. "Be right back, then."

He scanned the menu, made his way through the fast-moving line and placed his order. Natalie kept her gaze down as he approached and slid into the booth beside her. Her sharp intake of breath was the only reaction he got.

"I heard Cowtown's rodeo queen is stepping down." He turned to face her. "Will that mess up your campaign?"

"Yeah, I heard. It'll definitely put a kink in things." Her

sigh sounded frustrated. "They can't seem to keep anyone, and I don't understand why."

"Most single women want to keep Friday and Saturday nights open for dates." Caitlyn shot her a grin.

"Didn't you and Caitlyn used to race barrels?" He set his hat on the table. "One of you should apply."

"From the looks of things—" Caitlyn's gaze cut from Lane to Natalie "—Natalie might want to keep her Friday and Saturday nights open."

"I don't think I could run a publicity campaign and serve as rodeo queen." Natalie shot her sister a look. "Besides, I only dallied at barrels. You were the serious one. You should apply, Cait."

"It actually sounds like fun. I'll think about it." Caitlyn polished off her salad and yawned. "I'm beat. I think I'll head on home if it's all the same to y'all."

"Me, too." Natalie squirmed, hinting at him to let her out.

"You've barely touched your salad. Stay put, keep Lane company. Buy his dinner. After all, he worked on your fence today."

"No need for that. I already paid when I ordered. But I wouldn't mind the company."

Caitlyn slung her purse over her shoulder and stood. "Y'all have fun."

Steam billowed off Natalie as Caitlyn hurried out the door.

Would she ever enjoy being near him? His stomach took a dive.

"So, did you finish the fence?" Her voice came out tight.

"Just the posts. The concrete has to set. I kept hoping you'd get home to approve before I left, but I finally gave up."

"I'm sure it's fine. I can't complain about a fence built for free, now, can I?"

"Once we finish the photo shoot tomorrow, I'll be back to do the railing."

The waitress brought his Philly cheesesteak sandwich, the plate piled high with onion rings.

"Thanks." He bowed his head and said a quick prayer, then sank his teeth into the tender sandwich.

Natalie stared at him.

"What?"

"You prayed."

"Yep."

"Caitlyn did, too. I guess I should do that before I eat now, huh?"

"Natalie." An older version of Natalie stopped beside their table. The man with her wore a father's frown.

Natalie's face flamed. "Hi, Mama. Daddy."

"Who's your friend?" The man's voice was as tight as Natalie's.

"This is Lane Gray. We went to high school together. Lane, meet my parents—Daniel and Claire Wentworth."

"Nice to meet you both." Lane reached to tip his hat, then remembered he'd shed it and Caitlyn had moved it into the seat beside her before she'd left.

"Lane's building a fence around my backyard, so Caitlyn suggested I buy him dinner. She joined us, but she left already."

"It's a pleasure to meet you, Lane." Natalie's mom winked. "Y'all have fun." Sure seemed like a gesture of approval. But her dad was another story. He walked away with a glower and cast suspicious glances in Lane's direction as he moved through the line. After placing their orders, her parents sat in a booth directly across the aisle from him and Natalie.

"If you don't mind—" she drained her tea "—we've got an early photo shoot tomorrow and I can't take the scrutiny a minute longer. Could you let me out, please?"

Lane stood and stepped aside. "Another time, maybe?"

She wouldn't meet his gaze. "Thanks for the fence. I'm

sure Rusty will appreciate it. Be sure and send me a bill for supplies when it's done."

"Sure." Maybe he'd hand deliver it. Probably wouldn't see her after the shoot tomorrow. Obviously, he'd have to create every opportunity to see her. She certainly wasn't going to help him any in his pursuit.

And pursuing Natalie Wentworth's heart might just be the hardest challenge he'd ever faced. But she was well worth the effort and the pursuit was well worth the prize.

She walked out the door. Hair prickled at the back of his neck. He turned to meet the hard stare of her dad.

Lord, I need an ally.

Her mom smiled.

Lane tried to act natural. It should be easy. He was at home in the arena at Cowtown Coliseum with the smell of manure, horseflesh and bovines. Yet the flash of the camera distracted him. But not as much as Natalie did.

"It's almost like old times." Rayna, the creative director for the publicity campaign—whatever that meant—supervised from the box seats.

Kendra kept her huge lens focused on him. "You're doing great, Lane. You're a natural."

He felt anything but natural. Especially with Natalie standing on the second rail of the fence nearby with her arms hooked over the top—watching his every move.

Just a glance at her turned him into a quivering mass.

"That's enough riding fences, let's get some of your horse," she called.

As if he needed a reminder of her presence.

"Today's a great start for the ads and the website, but we'll have to set up another day to get more shots."

"More?" he whispered under his breath as he sauntered toward his horse.

"I heard that. Why do men always complain about having their picture taken?"

He probably wouldn't if she'd go away. Maybe he could relax. "I'd think the dozens Kendra's already taken would suffice."

She propped her hands on her hips. "Obviously you've never been involved in a publicity campaign."

"Can't say that I have." He lowered his voice. "Can't say I'd wanna do it again either."

"I heard that."

But then, at least he was getting to spend time with her. He smiled.

"See, now you're getting the hang of it."

He could definitely get the hang of hanging out with her. Now, if he could just hang out with her—and think. At the same time.

Natalie turned into the long driveway leading to Lacie and Quinn's ranch. The last time she'd been here she'd been uninvited and asked to leave. But not today.

May warmed the temperature to the low eighties. With her windows down, strands of hair escaped her braid and whipped about, sticking to her lipstick.

Perfect weather for a trail ride. Not too hot, not too cold. Perfect for her first Wyatt-approved time with Hannah.

All moisture evaporated from her mouth. Several pickups lined the parking area near the large ranch house. Couples gathered at the barn. A few kids were scattered here and there. Her gaze scanned the group for Hannah.

There she was—holding Star's hand. A vise clenched around Natalie's heart. Her eyes stung.

Hold it together. No scenes. No upsetting her daughter. She'd promised. And if it killed her, she'd keep that promise.

She sucked in a big breath, opened her car door and headed for the barn.

Wyatt scowled at her from his seat atop a bay horse. The mare's mahogany coat gleamed and her black tail swished, alert and ready just like her rider.

"Natalie. Over here, I've got Susie saddled for you." Lane's voice sent a shiver through her.

Lane?

Her steps stuttered. Who invited him?

He stood near the barn with her gray-and-white Appaloosa. She couldn't seem to get away from him. At work, at home, at play. He keyed her all up and she needed to be calm today. Pull it together.

Mustering up all the confidence she could gather, she strode toward her horse. "Hey, girl, I missed you." She stroked the mare's silky face. Her horse nuzzled her hand in return.

"I'd say she missed you, too." Lacie held Hannah while Star mounted her golden palomino.

"Say hi to Natalie, Hannah." Star settled in her saddle. "She's a friend of ours."

Natalie let her gaze settle on Hannah.

"Hi, Natawee."

Her heart hitched. Her eyes scalded.

"We're glad Natalie could join us today." Star smiled.

Lacie handed Hannah up to Star, and Natalie's arms ached to hold her daughter.

"You're doing fine," Lane whispered. "How about getting on your horse? We'll lead the ride, so you can keep your back to everyone and get your emotions in check."

On autopilot, she swung into her saddle. Lane was astride his sorrel in moments and rode up beside her. Natalie clicked her tongue and snapped the reins. Susie surged forward. Lane's rust-colored mount with its creamy mane and tail barreled ahead.

Indian blanket wildflowers lined the trail with their daisy-shaped, vibrant scarlet centers, orange petals and yellow tips. The horses' thundering hooves sent birds into panicky flight and unseen creatures scurrying deeper into hiding. The clear blue sky spread into infinity above with blinding sunlight. Sweat trickled down her back.

The trail narrowed and the horses were neck and neck. Natalie reined her horse to slow down.

Lane fell in behind her. "You okay?"

"Yeah." Her voice didn't crack. The extra moisture in her eyes had dried.

"It'll be a bumpy ride. But, eventually, maybe you can get closer to her."

"I hope so. But I can't talk about that if I'm gonna hold it together." Why couldn't he leave her alone? She really didn't need any added complications today.

"All right then—change of subject. How about them Cowboys?"

"No one's bothered me since your little show the other day. They all think we're an item."

"Good." Lane laughed. "But I meant football."

"Oh. I'm not into sports."

"Okay, what are you into?"

"Seeing my daughter grow up. I think I'm okay, now. I'd like to slow down and get closer to her."

He slowed his horse. "I'm right here if you need me."

Her heart twisted. She did need him. Almost as much as she needed Hannah. How had Lane wrangled his way back into her heart when they could never be?

The other riders caught up. She fell in stride beside Hannah and Star, while Lane stayed distractingly close behind her. She'd had enough one-on-one with Lane to last her a lifetime.

"So, you like horses, Hannah?" Natalie shot her daughter a bright smile.

"I lub Buttacweam."

"That's Buttacweam you're riding?" She mimicked her daughter's cute mispronunciation.

Hannah set both hands on her hips. "It's Buttacweam."

"Oh, Buttercream." She nodded. "I've had Susie for about four years, but I haven't spent much time with her lately."

"Susie is Unca Quinn's horsey."

"No, she belongs to Natalie." Star tightened her hold on the child. "Natalie moved away from Aubrey for a while, so Uncle Quinn boards Susie for her."

"Why you move?" Hannah frowned.

Natalie searched for a rational reason to spend a minute away from this enchanting child, much less a year and a half.

"A job." Star smiled. "Natalie got to work at Six Flags."

"My fav'wit." Hannah bounced in the saddle.

"Mine, too. When I was little I wanted to grow up to be one of those girls who get to roller skate around Six Flags all day and sweep up trash."

Hannah's eyes widened. "You did?"

How to explain publicity to a child? "But I got to do something a lot more fun. I got to tell people how cool it was, so they'd come see for themselves. What's your favorite ride there?"

"Tweety's fewwis wheel."

"I love Tweety."

"Maybe next time you go to Six Flags, Natalie can come, too." Lane suggested.

Natalie had almost forgotten he was right behind her. Almost. "I'd love to go with you, Hannah."

"Let's slow it down a little," Wyatt barked.

Natalie's heart sank.

"We not too fast, Daddy."

"Faster than I'm comfortable with." He rode up beside Star. "Here, ride with Daddy awhile."

Wyatt scooped Hannah into his arms and surged to the front.

"Now we fast." Hannah giggled.

"You okay?" Lane rode up beside Natalie.

"Fine." She snapped the reins and shot ahead of him again. Wyatt was determined she wouldn't get too close to Hannah. And Natalie was determined not to get too close to Lane. Her heart couldn't take either challenge.

Lane hung around when they got back to the ranch house. Natalie had held it together all afternoon, but if she crumbled he wanted to be there.

"I've got lunch all ready. We just need to transport it to the picnic area out back." Lacie headed for the house.

Natalie followed toward the large cedar-sided house.

Wyatt stepped in front of her. "You're not staying for lunch."

Natalie blinked. Her gaze fell to the ground. "Of course."

"Come on, Wyatt." Lane hurried to her side.

"No, it's okay. We didn't discuss lunch." She bit her lip. "It's fine. I appreciate you letting me come today."

Star gave Natalie an apologetic look. "Hannah, Natalie's leaving, why don't you give her a hug?"

Wyatt shot his wife a murderous glare as she leaned the little girl toward Natalie.

Hannah's arms wound around Natalie's neck and Star let go of her. Natalie's eyes closed as her daughter clung to her. She snuggled Hannah close. A sweet smile curved her lips as tears rimmed her lashes.

"That's enough," Wyatt snapped.

Natalie's eyes opened; her smile disappeared. She dabbed at her tears and handed Hannah back over to Star.

"Thanks for inviting me." Her voice came out choked and she spun toward her car. "Bye, Hannah."

"Bye, Natawee."

Why hadn't he figured out a way to drive her over? She was in no shape to drive. Her car engine revved. At least her place wasn't far.

Lane jogged to his truck and pulled out behind her. She drove too fast, but was otherwise in control, stopping at all the stop signs. Still, Lane was relieved when she pulled into her drive. He followed.

"Why are you following me?" She slammed her car door shut.

"You're upset. I wanted to make sure you made it home okay."

"I'm not upset. I'm fine." But even as she said it, tears traced down each cheek. She dashed toward the house.

Lane sprinted after her.

Hands shaking, she jabbed the key at the lock. "I was okay. Until she hugged me." Lane pulled her into his arms, offering comfort.

She didn't resist. Her whole body shook, but she didn't make much noise as her tears soaked his shoulder. Minutes passed and she stilled, but stayed in his arms. Paradise.

He didn't say anything, afraid to break the spell, just enjoying the feel of her trusting him.

"How can it feel so great and so horrible to see her—all at the same time?" She pulled away from him.

His arms felt empty. Cold.

"Let's sit." He steered her to the porch swing.

She sank into the seat. "I mean—holding her hurt, but it was bliss."

Kind of like holding Natalie.

"It hurt because Wyatt's still being a jerk." Lane settled beside her. The chains creaked as they swayed back and forth. "If he'd lighten up, it wouldn't hurt so much."

"Wyatt's having a hard time. I've put him through a lot."

"You're defending him?" Lane turned toward her.

Her gaze stayed on her hands in her lap. "He doesn't have to let me see her at all. But he is."

"What kind of man takes a child away from her mother?"

"He didn't do that."

"Okay, it was a judge's ruling, then, but you're different now. Anyone can see that. If he'd just get over himself and take a good look at you, he'd see it, too. You should take him back to court."

She stood and hurried to the door. "You don't understand. You can't." She scurried inside.

Lane strode to the door. The deadbolt clicked into place. His fist was poised in midknock. She had let him into her life today as much as she was going to. For now.

Though everything in him wanted to camp out on her porch until she had to come out again, he turned toward his truck instead. Thoughts of her inside crying and alone tore at his gut. But he couldn't push his way into her heart. He had to earn his way there. If she wanted to be left alone, he had to respect that. For now.

Natalie stared out the window of her sunroom. Large trees graced the backyard and a slight breeze billowed the leaves. The completed white rail fence looked nice. Maybe she'd have someone fence in the front, too. But not Lane.

The light pouring through the windows onto the sunny yellow walls and white wicker with comfy, overstuffed pillows usually lightened her mood. But not today.

A cold nose pressed against her ankle. She mopped her face and scratched Rusty's ear. He clambered into her lap.

"Amazing Grace"—her new ringtone—played. She scanned the screen of her cell. Wyatt. She took a deep breath and tried to sound like she hadn't been crying. "Hi."

"Hey, Natalie. I called to apologize. Sorry for being difficult today. I should have let you stay for lunch."

"It's okay." She traced the phone with shaky fingertips. "I've put you through a lot, and I understand it's hard for you to trust me."

"I put you through a lot, too. And, for the record, Star didn't make me call. She did box my ears, but I decided to call and apologize on my own."

"I appreciate your letting me come at all." Her vision blurred.

"Your folks and Caitlyn are coming over after church for lunch tomorrow. How about you come along to make up for today?"

Her breath caught. "That sounds wonderful."

"You can come to church, too, unless you want to go with your folks."

Her heart skipped. "You don't mind me coming to y'all's church?"

"What kind of rascal would it make me if I didn't want you in church?" His smile sounded in his voice.

"Is anyone else coming to lunch?"

"Naw, just us and your family. Rayna's not involved, so she won't be doing any matchmaking."

How had he known who she meant? "Great. I'll see y'all then."

"What's going on with you and Lane, any—*ouch*. Um, strike that question. Star reminded me that it's none of my business. See you tomorrow, Nat."

Thank goodness she didn't have to try and explain Lane's presence in her life. Especially since she didn't understand it herself. "Thanks, Wyatt. I really appreciate it, and I promise I won't do anything to hurt Hannah. Ever."

"I'm beginning to realize that. Just know that if you do, you'll answer to me. Hope to see you in church."

She laughed. "There's irony in those last two statements."

"What? Oh." Wyatt chuckled.

They laughed together, then hung up. She and Wyatt laughing together—for the first time without the aid of alcohol.

"Thank You, Lord." As the unbidden words echoed in the empty room, Natalie realized it was the first time she'd thanked her newfound savior. For anything. She sank to her knees.

"Thank You for helping me be a new person. Thank You for fixing my relationship with my dad. Thank You for helping me to make my family proud for the first time in years." Tears ran down her cheeks. "Thank You for repairing my relationship with Wyatt. Thank You for giving me an unexpected ally in Star. Thank You for letting me see Hannah. Thank You for my little girl. Thank You for bringing Lane back into my life when I really needed him and for making him the man I've needed him to be." Her words stalled for a moment.

"If there's any chance for us, dear Lord, help me to tell him the truth about Hannah. And help him to accept my choices. The ones I made and the one I almost made." She sighed. "Never mind that, Lord. I shouldn't be praying over silly things like a relationship. Help me focus on You."

Lane strolled toward the sanctuary. He'd barely slept and had drank four cups of coffee already. He wasn't in the mood for small talk in the fellowship hall after Sunday school class and couldn't hold any more java before the service.

A brunette stepped through the glass doors. It was Natalie, looking like a bundle of sunshine in a modest yellow dress. And not sad, as he'd expected her to be after yesterday.

"Hey, Nat." He smiled. "I didn't expect to see you here looking so chipper."

"Me, neither. Wyatt called to apologize and invited me to

church. And I'm having lunch with them and my family afterward."

"That's great." Oh, to invite himself along for support. "I hope he'll behave."

"We had a nice talk. I think things are getting better between us."

"Good." Jealousy squeezed around his heart. No, Wyatt was married. Nothing to be jealous about. Or was there?

Were there any old feelings between Wyatt and Natalie that might resurface? Even if there were, she was a Christian now. But a new Christian.

"Why are you staring at me?"

Chapter 9

"I'm just glad you're here." Lane mentally lodged a boot to his own backside. *Stop second-guessing her. Pray for her, instead.* "Wanna sit with me?"

"I promised to sit with Kendra and Lacie. And I don't want Wyatt to think I'm still—like I used to be with men." Her face heated.

"We'll be in the same general area, anyway. I usually sit with Quinn, Clay or Stetson. Shall we?"

"Natalie!" Kendra hurried toward them and hugged Natalie. "I'm so glad you're here."

Stetson shook Lane's hand. "Good seeing you, Gray. I take it you like our church."

"I do. Planning to stick around and join today."

"Awesome." Stetson pressed his hand to his wife's back. "Ready to go in the sanctuary?"

"Go on, we'll be there in a jiff."

Natalie stayed with Kendra as Lane followed Stetson inside. Kendra would be a great influence on Natalie. He'd heard enough at the rodeo to know Kendra's past was similar to Natalie's. Maybe Kendra could help Natalie in her new Christian walk.

"Don't worry." Natalie smoothed a shaky hand over her hair. "Wyatt okayed my being here."

"Wyatt doesn't have to okay you being here." Kendra frowned.

"You know what I mean."

"Why didn't you stay for lunch yesterday at Lacie and Quinn's?"

"Wyatt didn't want me to."

Kendra's frown deepened. "Since when do you have to do what Wyatt wants?"

"Since Wyatt has control of our daughter's life."

"True." Kendra rolled her eyes. "But he's being a horse's heinie about it."

"Actually he called last night and apologized. He invited me to church today and to lunch at their house with the rest of my family afterward."

"Wow. Why the turnaround?"

"I think Star had something to do with it." Natalie bit her lip. "I never dreamed she'd be my ally. The first few times I met her—I got a few digs in at her, and I thought she was fake. I mean—surely no one could be that nice for real. But she is."

"Yes. She is. She loves Wyatt and she loves Hannah." Kendra crossed her arms over her chest. "Initially, even before you came back to town, Star was unsure of herself and of how Wyatt felt about you, me and his other past flings. But Wyatt convinced her she's the only woman for him. And she's spent lots of prayer time concerning you and Hannah since you've been back. She truly wants what's best. For everyone."

"I owe her."

"You do." Kendra sighed. "I think I wanna be her when I grow up."

Natalie smiled. "I think you're doing a pretty stand-up job of being the new you."

"I try. And fail. And try again." A family entered the lobby. Kendra greeted them and waited until they went into the sanctuary before she spoke again. "But I have an idea of how Star and Wyatt feel toward you."

"How?"

"Stetson and I adopted Danielle."

"I never knew that."

"It all happened when you were out of town. We knew the birth parents from the youth group." Kendra's voice shook. "Everything was fine until last year. Danielle's birth mother came to see her and her birth father was living and working too close for comfort. I worried constantly they'd take her away from us."

"I had no idea." Natalie sucked in a shaky breath. "You've been great for supporting me."

"I'm beginning to realize sometimes our trials equip us to help others. I can see both sides." Kendra shrugged. "And Wyatt really is a great guy now. He just still has that stubborn streak and his temper gets the best of him occasionally."

"Only occasionally?" Wyatt's voice came from down the hall.

"And he has big ears." Kendra grinned.

Natalie turned to face him. Star was with him, but not Hannah.

Wyatt clutched his heart, then tugged one of his ears. "I'm hurt. I never knew they were big." He shot Natalie a genuine smile. "Hey, Nat. Glad you could make it."

Her eyes burned. Maybe this could really work. Maybe she and Wyatt could be friends. She met Star's gaze and sent a silent "thank you." Maybe she and Star could even be friends.

They headed into the sanctuary.

"Morning, folks." Clay greeted them in his signature drawl. "I'm rounding up volunteers. Any ladies willing to make pies for the pie auction at the car show at the end of the month? All proceeds go to the Denton Vietnam Vets."

"Sure," Star and Kendra echoed. Each told him how many pies they'd bake as Clay took notes, then turned away.

"Hey," Natalie called.

He turned to her.

"Think I can't bake or something?"

"No. I..." Clay swallowed. "I wasn't sure you'd be sticking around."

"Well, I am. And it just so happens I make a mean blueberry pie."

He quirked an eyebrow. "Your grandma's mouthwatering recipe?"

"Sure as shooting."

"You'll need to be at the auction that Saturday in front of Moms. Starts at one. Each lady holds her pie while the bidding goes on. Drives up the price sometimes. Especially if she's caught the eye of more than one guy."

Her gaze strayed to Lane. Would he bid on her pie? Silly. Why would she want him to? "I can do that."

"How many?"

"Two."

He made a note. "Got you down. And Nattie, it's right nice seeing you in church. Glad you'll be sticking around."

"Come sit with us." Star squeezed her arm. "Hannah's in the nursery."

"Sure." She followed as they headed for their pew. Her gaze met Lane's. Where did he fit in her life? Or did he fit anywhere?

She sat between Kendra and Star—a good five bodies away

from Lane. Now, if her heart would just slow. And the erratic beat had nothing to do with Wyatt and Hannah.

Natalie couldn't stop staring across the oak table at Hannah. Such a sweet, loving child. She'd even sat on Natalie's lap for a few seconds in the living room. Just long enough to twist Natalie's heart into knots. But Hannah didn't stay anywhere very long. The longest she stayed anywhere was near Wyatt.

Natalie tried not to envy their bond. She had no right to. But her stomach pretzeled with thoughts of the relationship she could have had with her daughter if she hadn't been so self-centered.

"The meal was great." Daddy pushed his plate toward the center of the table.

"As usual." Caitlyn and Mama echoed each other.

Natalie blinked. Her family had eaten at Wyatt's home before. She'd missed so much back when she'd been trying to pretend Hannah didn't exist.

The house was homey, without the perfection of a professional interior decorator, but warm and inviting. No breakable knickknacks. Child friendly and filled with love. The perfect place for Hannah to grow up.

Star picked up several plates. Mama and Caitlyn stood to help.

"Let's go outside," Wyatt whispered.

Natalie's gaze met Star's. Star gave a slight nod.

"Am I leaving?" Natalie stood.

"No. I just want to talk to you."

Her insides wobbled. Had Wyatt changed his mind about letting her anywhere near Hannah? Was he easing her out of her little girl's life as he'd eased her in?

"We'll be right back." Wyatt squeezed Star's shoulder.

"Take your time." Star didn't even look up as she loaded plates in the dishwasher.

Natalie's knees went weak. Somehow, she managed to stay upright and follow Wyatt out the back door.

They rounded the house. Wyatt strolled to the porch and settled in a rocker there. He gestured to the one beside it.

She sat and concentrated on the neighborhood to quell the quaking inside. Dark-brick houses with large lots and interesting shapes made each home unique. It was different from most cookie-cutter subdivisions.

A *For Sale* sign she hadn't noticed before stood by the road. Her heart stalled. "You're moving?"

"Relax. Hopefully to Aubrey."

"Oh." She started breathing again. "I'll admit I never pictured you living in a subdivision." Natalie tried to sound casual, as if her world didn't hinge on Wyatt letting her see Hannah. Or not.

He laughed. "Me, neither. And I can't say I'm real happy here. This was Star's place. Since I was renting, we decided to move here. But I need wide open spaces."

"Is Star okay with that?"

"She's been a city girl all her life, but she loves the peacefulness of Lacie and Quinn's ranch, so I think it's grown on her."

"She's a wonderful person. I couldn't have asked for a better..." Her words stalled. "A better...mother for Hannah."

"Star keeps me grounded. When I fly off the handle, she calmly brings me back down to earth. She loves Hannah. And me. I don't know what I did to deserve her."

Natalie's gaze dropped to the wood-planked porch floor. "How does she feel about me in the picture?"

"She's the reason I went to the session with Brother Timothy. The reason I let you come to the trail ride. The reason you're here today."

"Have you changed your mind?" Her insides quivered. "Is this the last time I'll see Hannah?"

"'Course not. Why would you think that?"

She blew out a big breath as her soul settled. "I don't know. You wanted to talk to me. Star's not here to referee."

"We're Hannah's parents. We need to get along for her sake. Without a referee."

"Agreed."

"Star and I talked last night. We'd like you to come with your folks when they visit, be at their house when Hannah visits them and eventually have one-on-one visits with her. But for now, you're still just Natalie."

Her heart did giddy somersaults. "I'll take that offer."

"Friends?" He held his hand out toward her.

She'd never imagined they'd be friends. Memories of their past relationship coiled shame through her stomach. But that was a different life.

Natalie clasped his hand. "Yes."

The front door opened and Star stepped out. Her gaze landed on their joined hands.

Natalie pulled out of his grasp.

"Just wanted to make sure y'all were getting along okay." Star's smile was shaky.

"We're fine, thanks to you." Wyatt stood and hugged his wife.

"Could we talk a minute, Star?" Natalie tried to infuse warmth in her tone. "Wyatt, you're excused."

"I'm thinking I should stay." He ended the embrace, but his arm rested around Star's waist.

"I want to thank Star for being so kind to me."

He sized her up, clearly wondering if he could trust her. With a slight nod, he kissed Star's temple and went inside.

"I understand I owe my being here today, and any chance I have at being part of Hannah's life, to you."

Star sat in the chair Wyatt had abandoned, but didn't say anything.

"In return for your kindness, you come out on your front porch to find me holding your husband's hand."

"Am I a complete idiot?" Star shook her head. "Don't get me wrong—I trust Wyatt. Completely."

"But not me." Natalie shrugged. "You have every reason not to. But, Wyatt and I never loved each other."

A huge sigh escaped Star. "He's told me that. Over and over. But it's nice to hear it from you."

"I don't want Wyatt, and I'd never do anything to harm y'all's relationship. We called a truce. That's all. All I want is to be part of Hannah's life. And I won't try to take her. I couldn't if I tried."

Star closed her eyes for a moment. "I appreciate your relieving my fears."

"I appreciate your being so kind to me when I don't deserve it."

"You're Hannah's birth mother. What kind of person would I be if I didn't allow you into her life?"

"I don't know. But it makes you an awesome person to allow it." Natalie's gaze dropped to the floor. "Especially since I wasn't very kind to you in the beginning. I'll never be able to thank you enough."

"Just don't hurt her. Don't let her down."

"You have my word. That didn't used to be worth anything." Natalie rolled her eyes. "But I'm working on changing that."

"What about that guy—Lane? Where does he fit in?"

Natalie's heart swooned at the mere mention of his name. "It's complicated."

"I don't mean to be nosy, but I've seen y'all together. I don't want Hannah getting attached to you and then watch you get married or something and move away."

"There won't be any 'or something' in my life anymore. And I can't imagine getting married." She shrugged. Especially to Lane. "But if that ever happens, I'm not going anywhere. Hannah is my priority. It took me a while to catch on, but she's what matters most."

"Then we'd better get back inside and see about what matters most."

"Thank you." Natalie's voice caught. "For everything."

She stood and Star did, too. It was awkward for a moment until Star opened her arms. Hannah's two mothers hugged.

"Who'd have ever thought it?" Natalie laughed.

"God can mend hearts, relationships and make friends out of potential enemies. If we'll let Him." Star took her hand and they stepped inside.

Natalie just needed to focus on God. And Hannah. And forget Lane.

But that would be difficult. She had to work with him. At least two more photo shoots. She had to oversee his clothing choices from Caitlyn's store. And he'd joined the church this morning. Lane Gray was making himself hard to avoid.

Lane strolled the brick-lined street of the Fort Worth Stockyards. Almost a week had passed since he'd seen Natalie. He needed to figure out a way to see her in between weekends. Hopefully, she'd be at her sister's store. If not, maybe he'd come another day to get his new clothes. If he couldn't catch her there, maybe at the rodeo and church over the weekend. Surely he wouldn't have to wait a whole week until the photo shoot.

He shook his head. Think about something else.

As he dodged his way through the crowd, Brother Timothy's words from Sunday morning's announcements played over and over in his head. He'd asked the church to pray about hiring an associate pastor.

Associate pastor? Preaching? *Me?*

Lane had long felt God's urging for him to do something. But preaching?

Filling in when the pastor couldn't be there. Visiting. Taking some of the load off Brother Timothy. He'd even done a Google search about nearby seminaries. There was one in Fort Worth. Could he even be an associate pastor with his past?

He opened the door of Caitlyn's store and the bell jingled. Natalie stood at the counter. His steps stalled. His brain did, too.

"Hey. We've got all your gear choices on the west wall. Here's the list of everything you're supposed to get." She sorted through a file and handed him a paper.

Their fingers touched.

Electricity flared.

Her gaze shot away from his.

He scanned the list. "All this?"

"Cowtown orders."

"I'm terrible at this kind of stuff. Got any advice?"

"Where's Caitlyn when I need her?"

"Where is Caitlyn?"

"She's in the back unloading a new shipment. Cowtown management wanted me here to supervise the staff clothing." She stalked to the long wall. "Green's good on you. How about this?" Natalie held up a shirt.

Lane's gaze stayed on her.

"Hello?" She jiggled the shirt at him. "What do you think?"

"Suits me." Lane shrugged.

"What size? I don't think this one will fit across your, um…shoulders."

"You're right. I'll probably need an extra large."

"But that would be all baggy around your, um…middle. Let's try a large." She handed him a shirt. "Dressing rooms are in the back."

Why was she so nervous? Did his shoulders and middle

make her nervous? "It's just a shirt. I could try it on right here." He undid a couple of buttons at his throat.

Her brows went up. "No!"

"I hate dressing rooms. They make me claustrophobic." He really shouldn't toy with her. But it was way too much fun.

"Deal with it. You can't stand in the middle of a store and shed your shirt."

He shot her a grin. "'Fraid you might keel over?"

For a second, she looked as if she might.

"Please." Sarcasm slipped off her tongue. She rolled her eyes and flung the shirt at him.

He caught it and turned toward the dressing room.

"Pick all your shirts and jeans, too, so you can take it all to the dressing room at once. That way, you can get out of here quicker."

"Eager to get rid of me?"

"I've got a dozen staff members coming in today and four dressing rooms. I don't need you endlessly tying a room up."

"If all the other guys are coming in today, maybe I need to stick around. Make sure they don't try anything with my gal." He winked at her.

Natalie's cheeks pinked. "I'm not—"

The door opened. A chute boss from Cowtown sauntered in.

"Hey, Natalie. I'm supposed to see a gal about some clothes. I didn't know it was you." Jimmy looked her up and down.

Steam erupted in Lane's head.

Chapter 10

"Hey, Jimmy. How are you?" His words came out tight, clipped, as he stepped around a rack into the cowboy's line of vision and sidled close to Natalie. He slid his arm around her waist and pulled her against his side.

She stiffened.

"Don't miss me too bad, babe, while I make the rest of my selections and try this stuff on." He grazed her cheek with his lips and had a hard time stopping there.

She shivered, flipped through her file and handed Jimmy a paper. "Here's your list. All your choices are on the west wall."

Jimmy huffed out a sigh and turned away.

Natalie pulled away from Lane. But it was too late. He'd felt her reaction to him. He grinned.

It wasn't fair of him to use her physical reaction to him against her. But he'd use whatever advantage he had to get close enough to Natalie to win her heart.

* * *

When Lane got to the photo shoot, Natalie could see that his eyes matched the shirt she'd picked for him. Perfectly. Why did he have to be the ideal specimen of maleness? Muscle upon muscle of handsome cowboy. The shirt stretched across his broad shoulders, revealing his strength, but didn't camouflage his narrow waist and hips.

And why did she have to oversee the photo shoot? Kendra knew what she was doing. So did Rayna. That's why she'd convinced them to work with her on the campaign for the Cowtown Coliseum.

"What do you think, Natalie?" Kendra's voice broke into her musings.

She forced her gaze away from Lane. "About?"

Kendra raised a brow and grinned. "Do we have enough shots of Lane? Or did you need to see more of him?"

Her face warmed. She definitely wanted to see more of him. In spite of everything. "That's enough stills. But we need some live shots of our pickup man doing his job."

"I'm on it." Lane jogged toward the arena. Was he eager to escape her, too?

Natalie watched until he disappeared.

"I think you need to supervise the live action." Kendra shot her a knowing grin.

"I think you're right." Natalie rounded the stands in time to see a bronc careen from the chute. Wyatt sat astride it as Lane brought his horse in close. The buzzer sounded and Lane seamlessly helped Wyatt off the bronc and onto his horse. The bronc charged toward the gate as the chute boss opened it.

The chute boss she knew all too well.

"Am I done yet?" Lane trotted over to her with a glower on his face.

Had Jimmy said or done something to set Lane off? "What's wrong?"

"I didn't sign up for pretend rodeos."

"No, but you're Cowtown staff and we're here to promote the rodeo." She propped her hands on her hips.

"It's fake. But the broncs are real. I didn't think about it until we were out there, but someone could get hurt."

"That's why you're here. It's your job to make sure that doesn't happen."

"Trust me, pickup men can't always keep an injury—or worse—at bay." He winced. "It doesn't make sense to put a rider at risk for a camera. Can't you get your film at a real rodeo, when these guys are out here risking their lives anyway, instead of setting them up for an extra chance for injury?"

What he said made sense.

"I'm not trying to be difficult," he continued. "It's just—I've seen the damage a bronc can do to a man." His jaw twitched. "I reckon you're setting up a fake bull ride, too."

Natalie certainly didn't want to be held responsible if anything went wrong. "You're right. I'll talk to management and arrange a shoot next Friday night." She turned and called out to her crew. "That's a wrap. I'll get with everyone on the details before the next shoot."

The crew started breaking down their equipment.

Lane swung down from his horse. "I know this will prolong your job, but I appreciate it."

"I appreciate your concerns. You take your job very seriously."

"I have to. I don't need any more good men like Mel Gentry on my conscience."

"You can't blame yourself for Mel's death. He knew the risks."

"He did, and it was his choice. But I still can't get it out of my head." His voice cracked.

"I'm sorry."

"Yeah. Me, too." Lane led his horse out of the arena.

When had he become this selfless, caring man? A man she could trust with her heart? Could she trust him to handle her truth?

Natalie spotted a red 1940 Ford Coupe, a black '57 Chevy two-door hardtop, and a blue '69 Camaro among the antique cars in various colors and styles from numerous decades lining Aubrey's Main Street. Tractors and farm equipment rounded out the display, while Aubrey's own superstar, Garrett Steele—live and in person—crooned country love songs from the stage.

Her cousin Jenna would keep her distance until he cleared out of town. Why could none of the Wentworth girls manage to get over their high school sweethearts?

She caught a glimpse of Lane in the crowd. Butterflies zoomed around in Natalie's stomach. The pie auction seemed endless, with her pies up next.

Behind the auctioneer, Rayna held her pie. Clay bid against Rayna's dad until the price was up to two hundred dollars. For a pie?

Clay bought the first pie, then folded and let her dad have the second one.

"Our next pie—" the auctioneer paused to read from his list "—is blueberry. Actually, there's two of 'em made by Miss Natalie Wentworth."

A few catcalls echoed through the gathering. Her cheeks heated as she noticed a couple of all-too-familiar cowboys.

Lane glowered.

"Settle down, boys," Clay drawled.

"We'll start the bidding at one hundred dollars."

Lane raised his hand.

"Hundred dollar bid, now one-ten, now one-ten, will ya give me one-ten?" The auctioneer made the rhythmic chant sound effortless.

"One-ten," one of the catcalling cowboys called.

"One-fifty," Lane shouted.

Natalie's cheeks heated again.

"One-fifty bid, now one-sixty, now one-sixty, will ya give me one-sixty?" the auctioneer called.

One cowboy folded.

The other raised his hand. "One-sixty."

"Two-fifty." Lane bellowed.

Natalie's gaze flew to his.

He grinned and tipped his hat.

Her face steamed.

"Two-fifty bid, now two-sixty, now two-sixty, will ya give me two-sixty?" the auctioneer chanted, trying to up the bid.

The cowboy from her past looked down.

"Going once, going twice, sold to the young man in the green shirt."

The crowd applauded as Lane stepped forward to claim his pie. His fingers grazed hers as she passed it off to him.

"Hope you'll join me in a bit for pie." He winked at her.

Her face flamed.

"Now who'll start the bidding for blueberry pie number two?" the auctioneer called.

"Two hundred fifty," Lane shouted.

The crowd remained silent.

"Two-fifty bid, now two-sixty, now two-sixty, will ya give me two-sixty?"

Silence.

"Going once, going twice, sold to the same young man. I believe this boy likes blueberry pie. Or maybe it's the little lady behind the pie."

Natalie's face scalded.

Lane settled up with the cashier, grabbed his pies and offered his arm to Natalie. "There's a nice tree over there for eating pie under."

The crowd applauded as he pulled her away.

"What are you going to do with two blueberry pies?"

"Eat 'em."

"But you just spent five hundred dollars. On pie. It cost less than twenty bucks to make them both. I would have made you one for free."

"It's for a good cause. And it was worth every penny to get to eat pie with you."

Warmth curled through her stomach as he spread a blanket under a tree.

She sat down cross-legged and Lane joined her. Too close.

"Sorry about those guys. Keep hoping they'll grow up." He caught her hand in his.

Had he bought her pie for show? She pulled away.

"What?"

"You don't have to pretend." She gestured toward the crowd.

"There's no pretense in how I feel about you, Nat." He threaded his fingers through hers. "So, are you going to Brother Timothy and Sister Joan's twenty-fifth anniversary party?"

Her heart hammered so hard, surely he could hear it. "Planning to."

"We could go together?"

Her breath stalled. "Maybe."

"Wonder why they're having it at the Ever After Chapel instead of the church?"

"I heard Joan say that's where their wedding was." The Ever After Chapel. Her childhood dream. Lane and the Ever After Chapel. Her heart sped.

"What?"

"What, what?" Her gaze snagged on his.

"I can feel your pulse racing."

"Oh, um." She bit her lip. "The Ever After Chapel. I used

to dream of getting married there when I was a little girl." True. Not the reason her heart sped. But he didn't need to know all the details.

"I guess lots of little girls do." He forked up a piece of pie. "Open up."

"I can feed myself."

"Humor me. My grandparents always fed each other the first bite of pie."

Being with him like this—with him looking at her like that—took her breath away. Obediently, she opened her mouth. As the sweet berries exploded on her tongue, he handed her his fork and closed his eyes.

She fed him a bite. He sat there, chewing with his eyes still closed, moaning about how wonderful her pie was, with blueberries smeared on the corner of his lip. Oh, how she'd like to kiss the smear away.

Lord, can there be a future for us?

Going to church soothed Natalie. Who'd have ever thought she'd go on Sunday morning and evening, plus Wednesday night? By choice?

She smoothed her hands over the fluttery black skirt Caitlyn insisted she buy and hurried down the aisle of the sanctuary. No dillydallying in the lobby to give Lane time to show up, and she had to get a seat between friends so he couldn't sit by her. The feelings she'd had toward him lately needed to be doused. Especially after yesterday's pie incident.

How could she expect him to handle her truth when she didn't understand it herself?

Focus on God and Hannah. Period.

But Lane was already there. Beside Clay.

Natalie stopped. Maybe she'd sit somewhere else. No, with three couples seated, if she took the empty spot by Kendra there'd be several bodies between them. She hurried to the pew. Yes, Lacie or Star would sit beside her and everything would be fine. All the couples greeted her and Lane leaned forward to shoot her a brain-numbing smile.

"You okay?" Kendra whispered.

"Fine."

"You seem nervous. Is it Lane or Hannah and Wyatt?"

"Why does everybody think there's something between Lane and me?"

"We have eyes. He's always with you at the arena. And he bought your pies. For a lot of money."

She sighed. "It started out all for show. But now, I don't know."

"Huh?"

"Lane saw one of the cowboys hit on me. He decided to convince everyone we're an item so my former reputation won't haunt me."

"Oh. Well, I don't think it's for show anymore. Maybe it's just me, but he kind of looks like a lovestruck bull."

Natalie laughed. "Such a romantic image."

"Mind if I sit here?" Lane's baritone. Right. Beside. Her.

"Not at all." Her voice quivered right along with her insides.

The pianist began playing. People took their seats and the service began.

Natalie sang all the hymns with more fervor than usual as she tried to concentrate on anything but Lane. *Forgive me, Lord, for being so distracted.*

As Brother Timothy began his sermon, her brain settled. "Forgiveness. If we don't forgive others, how can we ever look Jesus in the eye when we get to glory?"

"Turn to Luke 23:34." Brother Timothy flipped through his Bible. "The letters in red—a cry from Jesus. 'Father, forgive them for they know not what they do.' Folks, while Jesus hung on the cross, people cast lots for His clothing, hurled insults at Him, and taunted Him to save Himself. And what did He do? He prayed for His father to forgive them. Who are we to hold sin against anyone? Much less ourselves?"

The words sank into Natalie's soul. God had forgiven her. For everything she'd ever done. Did He want her to forgive herself? For hanging out in bars and picking up men? For getting pregnant, for almost aborting and then abandoning Hannah?

The piano started playing. The altar call. She'd missed the end of the sermon. Pressure built in her chest with an overwhelming need to visit the altar.

"Excuse me." Natalie sidestepped Lane and four more friends, and went forward.

She knelt at the altar. Yes, God had forgiven her and He wanted her to forgive herself. "Lord, I need help to forgive myself. I've done so many bad things. And I knew about You. Forgive me for turning my back on You and the way You wanted me to live. Help me to live the way You want me to, to make the right choices and to overcome temptations from my former life. Give me strength and wisdom."

A weight lifted from her shoulders. She stood and hurried back to her pew. Instead of climbing over everyone again, she stood at the end beside Wyatt.

The service ended and people began filing out of the pews and toward the lobby.

"I'm proud of you." Wyatt hugged her.

"For?" A totally platonic hug from the father of her child. It felt good.

"Turning your life around."

"Me, too. But I think God did the turning."

Star gave her a quick hug and her other friends filed past. She stood at the end of the pew, clutching the rail, weak-kneed at the changes washing over her.

"I hope you'll be careful." Lane's voice shot a shudder through her.

"In what way?" She met his gaze.

"In your relationship with Wyatt."

All the peace Natalie had only just discovered melted away as her insides boiled.

Did he honestly think she'd try to come between Wyatt and Star to get closer to Hannah?

"How dare you? I'd never—" But in the past, she might have. "Okay, maybe I wasn't above marriage busting at one time. But I am now, and who made it your business anyway?"

"That's not what I meant." He swallowed hard. "But I know for a fact that sometimes feelings resurface when you least expect it. I don't want you to get caught up in anything."

"Why don't you worry about what you get caught up in and stay out of my life?" She jabbed a finger in his solid chest. Muscle upon muscle. Why had she touched him? She stalked out of the church.

Chapter 11

Still steaming, Natalie turned into her driveway. A gray truck. Wyatt's truck in her driveway? Wyatt sat on the porch steps. Star and Hannah were in the truck.

She parked in the garage, got out and hurried to meet him. "Is something wrong?"

"I made a decision."

Her stomach twisted. They'd been getting along well. Surely it wasn't bad. "Am I going to like it?"

"I think we should tell Hannah who you are. It'll be less jarring for her now, while she's young."

Bubbles burst inside Natalie. "That would be awesome. When?"

"Now? And I think if she wants to, she can stay here a few hours this afternoon. Unless you have something else going on."

"I don't, but if I did, I'd cancel."

"I'll go get her."

Her insides fluttered as if thousands of butterflies took flight. "Wait. What are we going to tell her?"

"The truth. Just follow my lead. She's young. She won't understand everything at first. And it probably won't be as big a deal to her as it is to us." He scrubbed a hand against his jaw. "I don't know what she should call you."

"Natalie is fine. Or we can let her decide."

"As long as Star has dibs on Mommy."

A knife jabbed her heart. But Star had earned the title. Natalie hadn't. "No problem. Was it Star's idea to tell her?"

"No. Came up with it all on my own."

"Is she okay with it?"

"Yes."

"All right." Natalie smoothed a hand over her skirt. "How do I look?"

Wyatt grinned. "Right pretty. You clean up good."

"Thanks. You do, too."

He turned toward his truck. Seconds later, Hannah was perched in his arms, and Star climbed down from the truck. As they walked toward Natalie, her whole body shook.

Hannah's eyes grew wide. "Natawee has big house. Like Aunt Caitlyn's and Grammy's."

"Let me show you around." Natalie held out her hand.

Wyatt set Hannah down on the porch and her small hand slid into Natalie's. Nerves prevailed as she gave a tour. Thankfully, her parents' housekeeper made daily visits and everything was in place.

Finished with the second floor, they came back down the stairs. "When I was a little girl, I grew up in Grammy's house. It was based on a dollhouse Grammy had when she was a little girl. When Caitlyn and I were little, we played with the dollhouse and when we grew up, we each got a life-sized dollhouse."

"It's pwetty." Hannah squeezed her hand tight as they descended.

"Thanks. My cousin is an interior decorator."

"What's that?"

"Someone who makes houses pretty."

"Hannah, we brought you to Natalie's to tell you something." Wyatt scooped the little girl into his arms. "You know how Caitlyn is your aunt and her parents are Grammy and Grand."

"Uh-huh." Hannah's pigtails bounced as she nodded.

"That's because Natalie is your mother."

Hannah thought for a moment, then looked at Star. "That's Mommy."

"You're right." Wyatt's tone remained patient. "Mommy is your mommy, but Natalie is your mother."

Natalie's eyes burned. She blinked. "Can I try?"

Wyatt nodded.

"Come sit by me." Natalie sat on the bottom step and patted the seat beside her.

Wyatt set Hannah down on the step.

"When you were a baby, I couldn't take care of you like I wanted to, so Daddy took you home from the hospital. He took care of you and when he married Star—she became your mommy."

Hannah frowned. "Were you sick?"

Sin sick. "Sort of. But I'm better now. And I'd like to spend more time with you."

"I live with Daddy."

"Yes, sweetpea." Wyatt knelt in front of Hannah. "You'll always live with me and Mommy."

"And you can visit me." Natalie put her arm around Hannah's slight shoulders. "And you can still call me Natalie, or whatever you want to call me. But Star is—" her voice cracked "—Mommy."

"Would you like to stay here with Natalie for a while?" Star's eyes were damp.

"Can I see the puppy?"

"Definitely. Let's go see the puppy." Natalie stood. "Maybe you can help me teach him not to jump on people. But before we do that, can I have a hug?"

Hannah hurled her little body into Natalie. Natalie scooped her up. Baby shampoo and innocence in a warm little bundle of love and acceptance.

If only adults were as resilient as children. To take what comes and not worry or dwell on it. Just go play with the puppy.

The puppy Lane had gotten her. To help her overcome her fear. Because he cared about her. He'd protected her from the leering cowboys because he cared about her.

And this morning, he'd cautioned her to be careful in her relationship with Wyatt. Because he cared about her. In light of her past, he had every right to worry about her intentions, but had she taken his warning wrong?

She needed to come clean with Lane. Test the waters and see if he felt the same way. Could they have a future together? Could he handle her truth?

"I love puppies." Hannah squirmed out of the embrace.

Natalie set her daughter down. *I love you.* Maybe someday soon, she could say it out loud.

Lane parked his truck behind the Coliseum and opened the horse trailer gate. The big dun backed out steadily, as she'd done thousands of times. He patted her flank. "Good girl, Rowdy."

If only he could handle female humans as well as he handled his horse. Seeing Natalie at the altar, at church on Sunday for both services and on Wednesday evening had been great—except that she was mad at him. And why shouldn't she be? She'd thought he was accusing her of trying to bust up Wyatt's marriage.

And only because he'd gotten jealous at their closeness and run off at the mouth.

He slipped Rowdy's bridle and halter into place. Maybe he'd joined the church too soon. He loved the people there and felt like Brother Timothy needed him there. But maybe he needed to distance himself from Natalie. He'd been so sure they were meant to be, but after weeks of trying, he'd gotten nowhere with her.

After tonight's rodeo, he shouldn't have to work with her anymore. At least, tonight wasn't one-on-one with her. He entered the Coliseum and led Rowdy to her stall.

Natalie was already there, talking with the camera crew. She laughed and joked as if all were right in her rodeo. If only he could be part of her rodeo. She saw him and grinned.

Huh? Wasn't she mad at him? His heart flipped over. His jaw went slack.

She headed in his direction.

Surely she'd pass him. There was probably someone behind him she'd smiled at. *Big oaf—at least close your mouth.*

"Hey." She stopped in front of him and stuffed her hands in her pockets. Almost shy. Was he in the Twilight Zone?

"Hey," he said. "Look, I'm sorry about what I said at church."

"It's okay. Really."

"No, it's not. It's none of my business."

"You were trying to help me." She lifted one shoulder. "The old Natalie would have stolen Wyatt from Star, gotten him to sign custody over, nabbed Hannah and dumped him. But I realize that's not what you meant."

"You do?"

"Wyatt and I never loved each other, so there are no feelings that might resurface."

His insides warmed. She'd never loved Wyatt. He'd never loved her.

A rowdy crowd of cowboys sidestepped them, joking and laughing.

She waited until the noise died down and moved closer to him. "Wyatt let me tell Hannah who I am. She spent Sunday afternoon with me. And we set up a visitation schedule."

Her nearness cut into his oxygen supply. "That's great. I'm glad he's doing the right thing. How did Hannah take the news?"

"Like a child." She grinned. "She just wanted to play with the puppy you got me. Which got me to thinking."

"You don't want him?"

"No, I do. I was thinking how kind you've been to me since I came back to town." Her gaze settled somewhere near his throat. "You've been very supportive. You tried to referee Wyatt and me when I first tried to see Hannah. You protected me from unwanted male attention. You got me a dog and built me a fence. Why did you do all that?"

"I hurt you once. I wanted to make up for it." That's how it started out, anyway.

"Is that all?"

I love you. Have since high school. "What are you getting at, Nat?"

"I've been having these feelings." The corner of her bottom lip tucked under her teeth. "And I wondered if you had any."

Was she saying what he thought she was saying? Or did his heart just hope? "Feelings for you?" He took a step closer to her.

Her gaze finally met his. She closed the gap between them and slid her arms around his neck.

His arms encircled her waist. He couldn't breathe for a solid minute. "It's more than this. For me, anyway. I hope it is for you, too."

"What is it, then?"

"I definitely think we should spend more time together and figure it out."

"Me, too."

"Brother Timothy and Sister Joan's anniversary party is Saturday. Still want to go? With me?"

"Definitely."

"It's a date. But right now, I gotta get my brain back in the arena." His gaze locked on her lips. "And I can't do that if you stick around."

She pulled away from him.

But his arms weren't ready to let go. He grabbed for her.

Natalie wagged a finger at him just out of his reach. "Uh-uh. I won't take the blame for a rodeo accident. Get your head back in the game, cowboy."

She turned away and left him standing there begging for more. A lifetime of more.

Natalie clutched Lane's arm and hoped her panty hose wouldn't slip any farther down. She scanned the Ever After Chapel reception room. The Holstein-spotted couch and gleaming tile floors set the tone for down-home gatherings.

They'd traversed the reception line to congratulate the pastor and his wife, then mingled with friends and other church members.

Would this be her only visit here with Lane? She had to tell him the truth. Soon. Things were moving forward between them at breakneck speed.

"Did I tell you you're beautiful?" he whispered near her ear.

And stole her breath. "A few times."

An orchestra began playing fancy music. She didn't recognize the song. Soft and lilting. Beautiful.

Her panty hose slipped down again. They'd been slipping with each step, but if she sat down, surely they'd stop. Thankfully, her dress came to the knee, but at the rate they were going…another step, another slip.

They were inside the reception room, and the panty hose were around her upper thighs now. Why had she worn the stupid things?

"Can we find our table?"

"You okay?"

"Fine. Um, I'll stand over here, and when you find our names I'll join you."

He frowned. "You sure you're okay?"

"My feet hurt." Just can't walk much more at the moment. Major wardrobe malfunction.

"I can imagine, in those shoes. You sure look hot, though." He winked.

She shivered. And her hose slid down more. Please let their table be close.

Lane left her side and scanned the first row of tables. He moved to the second row, then motioned her over. She met him, keeping her thighs together as much as she could. Blasted slim hips and skinny legs couldn't even keep a pair of panty hose up.

At least they were almost to the table.

He pulled her chair and she sank into it. Made it. Now she couldn't get up until the whole thing was over. Then maybe she could make a bathroom run. "You don't have to sit here with me. Go mingle."

"I'd rather be with you than anybody else here."

She leaned into his shoulder. "Ditto."

"I wish they'd open the dance floor. I'm dying for a chance to dance with you."

"Dancing?" Her panty hose definitely wouldn't survive a dance.

"What's wrong, don't you like to dance?"

"I do. But I…"

"Hey, Natalie." Kendra claimed the chair on her other side. "I finally finished taking pictures. Lane, can you go help Stetson and Clay move a few things back in place?"

"I'm on it." He squeezed Natalie's shoulder. "Be right back."

"You two seem cozy."

"For the first time in months, I'm having a hard time focusing on Lane."

"Why?"

"From the time I got out of his truck, my panty hose have been making a steady decline. They're just above my knees at the moment. Sadly, my dress isn't much lower."

Kendra giggled, then covered her mouth. "I'm sorry. I know it's not really funny."

"Actually it is, but I don't know what to do. I'm afraid if I get up, they'll be below my dress before I can make it to the bathroom."

"Take them off under the table. The tablecloth is long. No one will know."

"You think?"

"I'll warn you if anyone heads in this direction."

Natalie reached under the table. She slid her hose down quickly, then slipped her shoes off, pushed the left leg the rest of the way down with her right foot, and repeated the process with her free foot. She scooped up the loose hose with her toes, grabbed them and stuffed them in her purse. "Ah, much better."

"Perfect timing. Here come the guys." Kendra leaned near Natalie's ear. "And the panty hose caper will be our little secret."

Lane and Stetson joined them.

"Now that I've single-handedly solved the problems of the world, do you mind if we go now?" Kendra clutched Stetson's hand.

"You okay, doll?"

"Just tired from hauling myself around."

"Nothing to haul. You're one fine pregnant lady." Stetson helped her stand. "Our chariot awaits."

"'Night, y'all." Natalie waved them off.

"Miss Natalie, how are you?"

Natalie turned to see Brittany Miller behind her. "I'm fine. Sit with me. How are you?"

"Good." Brittany perched in the chair beside her. "I broke up with Jeff and I'm dating a really nice guy from our youth group now."

"That's wonderful."

"Thanks for your advice." Brittany's cheeks pinked and she lowered her voice. "I almost made a terrible mistake."

"Glad I could help."

"I better find my mom. I help out with small issues that pop up." With a shy wave, Brittany left their table.

"Who is Brittany?" Lane asked.

"She was in the Sunday school class my mom taught. She was about six then. I ran into her at Quinn and Lacie's wedding." It seemed like a lifetime ago. "Her boyfriend was pressuring her. I rescued her and tried to talk her out of giving in to him."

"I'm proud of you for helping her. For saving her from a jerk like I was once upon a time."

"It was a long time ago. You were a kid."

"A hormone with feet."

She laughed. "That, too."

Lane scanned the people milling about around them and pressed his lips near her ear. "What do you say we get out of here?"

She shivered. "Whenever you're ready."

He took her hand and led her outside.

Lane twined his fingers with hers and rounded the Ever After Chapel toward his truck. "I guess your feet recovered. You're walking better."

She bit her lip and sighed. Her face reddened. "This is so embarrassing. But my panty hose started slipping down the minute I got out of your truck."

Lane chuckled. "So that's why you squirmed around all night and could barely walk. That's quite a predicament you got yourself into, little lady."

"I'm glad you find my predicament funny. I guess I bought the wrong size." She cracked a smile. "I've never worn the stupid things before."

He chuckled again.

"I'm fine now. Kendra stood guard while I shimmied out of them under the table."

"If that wasn't so tantalizing an image, I'd laugh." He tugged at his collar. "If it's not something you usually wear, why did you?"

"I wanted to look…proper. For you."

Something inside him warmed and he brushed a soft kiss on her lips. "You're beautiful. And you look very proper. But you're definitely making me have improper thoughts."

A slight breeze stirred her hair. Her blue eyes glowed in the sunlight. It was increasingly hard to have proper thoughts about Natalie.

He stopped beside his truck but didn't open the door for her yet.

"Don't you need to get to the rodeo?"

"We've got a little time." He pulled her close. "I wanted you to myself for a bit."

"I'm not sure that's such a good idea." But she didn't resist and laid her head against his chest.

"You know those feelings we were discussing the other day?"

She pulled away enough to look up at him.

He could drown in her blue eyes. "I think I figured them out. I love you."

"Really?" Her eyes lit up and she did a little bounce in his arms. "I love you, too, Lane."

"I loved you back in high school. That's why I broke up with you. I was scared."

"You broke my heart back then, because I loved you. I still do."

"Oh, Natalie. So many wasted years." He kissed her—fully staking his claim, the way he'd wanted to for so long.

She moaned, cupping the back of his head with her hands as if she couldn't get enough of him.

With every ounce of strength he had, he grabbed her wrists and pulled away.

"What?" Her huge eyes questioned.

"We're going to do things right this time."

"I was just kissing you. That's all I wanted." She rolled her eyes. "Well, not all I wanted. But that's all I was going to do."

"But if you keep kissing me like that, I'm not sure it's all I'll do. I'm not feeling very Christian at the moment."

She took another step back. "You're right. We need to keep our heads, and besides—I need to tell you something."

"Me, too." What would she think of his imagined call? Would she want to marry him? Would she accept being an associate pastor's wife? Would she think he was crazy for entertaining the idea when she knew exactly what he'd been? "Let's talk after the rodeo."

"I'll be waiting." She kissed her palm and pressed it against his cheek. "I love you."

A shudder moved through him. "And I love you."

He opened the door and helped her into his truck.

Natalie Wentworth loved him. *Thank You, Lord.*

Nothing could dim the fire in Lane's soul. Not the manure-scented arena. Not the occasional foul language that peppered the air. Not painful memories from the past. He saddled his horse with a song in his heart. Put there by Natalie.

"Heard the latest rumor around the arena?" Wyatt's voice came from behind him.

"Don't care to."

"Me, neither, but it concerns you."

Lane turned to face him. "Keep talking."

"That you and Natalie are sleeping together."

Okay, maybe he'd been wrong. His chest boiled over and he clenched his fists. "That's none of your business. But no, we're not. Natalie's not like that anymore, and neither am I. For your information, I've only kissed her twice since high school. And that's all I've done."

"Simmer down, Gray." Wyatt clapped him on the shoulder. "Just telling you what I heard. I'm glad it's not true. But there's definitely something between y'all."

"We love each other and I plan to marry her."

"I'm glad. Natalie deserves something real based on love for a change. Lord knows, I treated her wrong." Wyatt offered his hand.

Lane clasped it. "I'm glad you let her come clean with Hannah, that you're letting Nat see her more often."

"Out of the mistake me and Natalie were, we got Hannah. We have to do right by her. Maybe the good Lord knew it would take something as big as parenthood to straighten us out."

"She's a special little girl. Takes after Natalie."

"True. Truth be told, I was a bigger mess than Natalie was, way back when. God definitely worked a miracle with me. Who'd have ever thought I'd talk Natalie out of an abortion and raise Hannah myself?"

The air went out of Lane's lungs. Abortion? Natalie had wanted to abort Hannah?

"Don't know what to do about the rumor, but I'm glad

you're treating her right." Wyatt clapped him on the back. "I better get going. Got a bull to ride in a few."

Lane leaned against the wall as if someone had sucker punched him.

Natalie's gaze never left Lane as he worked the arena. The buzzer sounded and he scooped a rider safely to the ground, then herded the bronc to the gate and faded into the background. The ghost of the arena. Many spectators didn't notice pickup men, since the rider took center stage.

The next bronc bucked into the arena, and Lane went on alert. As soon as the buzzer sounded, he moved in for the rescue. The cowboy yanked with both hands as his boot caught in the stirrup. Natalie cringed. If he fell, the horse would drag him.

The other pickup man crowded the bronc to slow it, while Lane loosed the rider. The cowboy landed on his feet and limped from the arena as Lane corralled the bronc to the gate. Her camera crew got it all. This was much better than a staged shoot.

"Next up, bull riding." Quinn Remington's voice echoed through the arena.

A red Brahman bull careened out of the chute with Wyatt astride. The hump-necked bull spun, lurched and changed direction, but Wyatt stayed on. He'd probably win tonight's event and the title this year. Though Saturday-night rodeos at the Stockyards weren't sanctioned for the Horizon Series road to the championship, it was work for Wyatt with a nice purse at the end of the evening.

The buzzer sounded and Wyatt tumbled off. The bull whirled around to charge him. Stetson, in full bullfighting gear, cut in front of the Brahman as Lane lassoed the bull and tugged the beast toward the gate.

Wyatt climbed the fence and leaped out of the arena. She'd

never really thought about his safety before. But this was Hannah's father. Hannah needed him. *Thank You, God, for bullfighters and pickup men. Thank You, God, for Lane.*

Her heart warmed. Surely he'd understand the mistake she'd almost made. They loved each other, and their future looked bright. Would he ask her to marry him?

The final round of bulls wrapped up. Happily ever after with Lane. Maybe even a baby. One she and Lane would raise. A sibling for Hannah.

Natalie stood and descended to the walkway around the arena toward the gate where staff exited as Quinn made final announcements and closed out the rodeo.

Eager to see Lane, she tapped her foot to the twangy music blaring from the speakers. The bullfighters exited, and the judges, and finally she caught a glimpse of Lane. Frowning.

Was he still upset about her camera crew? He saw her and his steps stalled for a second. Then he stalked toward her, anger brewing in his gaze and the taut lines of his jerky movements.

What was wrong with him? He was certainly upset about something.

"Ready to follow me home, cowboy?" She held her hands up in an innocent gesture. "I totally didn't mean anything by that. I thought we could sit on the porch, under the stars, and talk. Just talk."

He kept frowning.

"Lane?" She touched his arm.

He jerked away from her. "I guess now you're gonna tell me?" His words came out in a harsh whisper.

"Tell you what?"

"That you wanted to kill Hannah. That's what."

Chapter 12

Natalie's world shifted sideways. Her stomach lurched. "Who told you that?"

"Wyatt." Lane's green eyes blazed. "And I think he'd know the truth. Unlike me."

"Wyatt?" They'd been getting along well. Why would he hurt her like this?

"He thought I knew. We were just talking. He was actually bragging on you for not doing it." His laugh held a hollow, sarcastic ring.

She ran a finger across his cheek. "I was going to tell you. Tonight. That's what I wanted to talk to you about."

He batted her hand away. "It's a little late, don't you think?"

"Let me explain. Please."

"Save it." He stalked away.

Natalie watched him go, though everything in her wanted to jump on his back and hang on for dear life.

But hanging on to Lane wouldn't do any good. She'd lost him.

Her legs threatened to buckle, but she managed to make it out the exit and to her car. She didn't scan the parking lot for Lane, but jammed her key in the ignition and revved the engine. Horns blared as she cut into traffic without waiting her turn.

Natalie drove blindly with tears streaming down her face. She'd go back to her apartment in Garland. Away from Lane. But she couldn't. Hannah was in Denton, only fifteen minutes away. And Wyatt might move her to Aubrey. She couldn't tell Hannah she was her mother and then move an hour away. She couldn't let Hannah down. Again.

A horn blared. She jammed her brake, barely missing a car's fender as it shot across the intersection in front of her.

"What are you doing?" she shouted at the car.

Wait a minute—did she just run a red light? Natalie turned into a gas station, pulled around beside the quick mart and laid her head on the steering wheel.

A sob rose within her. She had to stay close to Hannah. No matter what it did to her heart. Maybe she'd move to Denton. That would get her away from Lane. Since she'd finalized her publicity plan, she could work from home now. And never see Lane Gray again.

A knock on glass sounded beside her. She jumped.

Kendra stood outside her window.

With shaky fingers, Natalie pushed every button she could find until the window finally slid down.

"Are you okay? You ran that red light."

"I know."

"What's wrong? Maybe you shouldn't be driving."

"I'm fine."

"Obviously you're not. Did something happen tonight?"

"I almost had it."

"What?"

"A happily ever after. With Lane." Her voice cracked. "I'd forgotten I ever wanted a happily ever after."

"Y'all had a fight."

"It's over."

"Maybe not. I thought it was over with Stetson once, and look at us now."

"No, it's over. Trust me. But, I'm okay. Y'all go on home."

"I'm not letting you drive yourself home. You're in no shape. Scoot over. I'll drive you. Stetson can pick me up at your place."

In her short friendship with Kendra, Natalie had learned enough to know it wouldn't do any good to argue. She climbed over the console and into the passenger's seat. "You're a good friend."

"Definitely. You have no idea what it's like for a rapidly growing, six-months-along pregnant lady to fold herself into a sports car." Kendra settled into the car and raised the steering wheel away from her swollen abdomen.

Natalie laughed, but it turned into tears.

Sunday morning already. Lane leaned against the tree in his backyard. The little stake cross stood tall with a recent fresh coat of paint.

After he'd finally told Brother Timothy about his former girlfriend's abortion, the pastor suggested he set up a monument to help him heal. Lane didn't know about healing, but it seemed like the place to go when life took a rough turn.

Natalie hadn't lost custody of Hannah. She hadn't wanted her. Had almost killed her. Why hadn't he seen the truth?

Because Natalie hadn't told him.

He kicked at the gravel and sent it flying across the yard. The bitterness and grief he'd felt toward his former girlfriend wound around his anger toward Natalie, smothering Christian thoughts of forgiveness. He probably shouldn't go to church. Definitely not in the mood. But in the past, he'd realized that when he didn't want to go—that's when he needed to most.

Lane stalked around the house to his truck, got in and started the engine. "Rock of Ages," the classic hymn, played on the radio. His churning soul settled. Yes, he definitely needed to be in church.

He passed Natalie's drive. Would she be in church today? Maybe he did need to find a new one.

A few miles later, he turned into the church parking lot. No sign of her blue Challenger. And she'd mentioned attending Sunday school soon. Though he dreaded seeing her, he'd hate for her to drop out of church because of him.

Just in time for class, he strolled through the sanctuary to his regular pew and claimed his seat beside Stetson.

Kendra leaned forward. "Natalie's going with her mom and dad to their church," she whispered. "I don't know what happened with y'all, but she nearly killed herself running a red light last night."

His heart lurched. "Is she okay?"

"Physically—yes. Thank God she didn't wreck."

Lane didn't respond.

"Y'all need to get over yourselves and get together."

"Kendra." Stetson's tone cautioned.

"Just saying. I mean it's obvious they're in love. And people who are in love should be together. Not apart and miserable." She shrugged. "But don't mind me. What do I know about happily ever after?"

The pianist began playing and a deacon stood to give the devotion.

Lane didn't hear any of it. He had to stop thinking about Natalie. No distractions. Focus on God and decide if he was crazy for thinking about the associate thing.

A prayer closed the devotion and the congregation scattered to their classes. Lane headed to the office. The door was open. Brother Timothy sat at his desk.

Lane tapped on the door frame. "You got a minute?"

"Sure. Come in."

He closed the door since he preferred that no one overheard.

"What's on your mind?"

"Several things. One, I'm not sure I should have joined this church."

"Why?"

"Natalie Wentworth and I were sort of seeing each other. It's over between us now, and I'm afraid she'll stop coming."

"Let's see—you're a member and she's not." Brother Timothy propped his elbows on the desk. "She goes with her mom and dad some, so maybe she'll go there, instead. Are you happy here?"

"Yes."

"Then wait and see. As long as Natalie goes somewhere, I don't think you need to leave. And she might not come here, whether you're here or not. What else?"

"The associate pastor thing."

"You have a recommendation?"

"I was thinking about going to seminary."

"Ah." Brother Timothy nodded. "That feeling you needed to do something?"

"Yes, I think God's tugging at me to preach."

"Congratulations."

"But I'm not sure."

"Because?" Brother Timothy steepled his fingers.

"My past."

"We all have things in our pasts."

"I told you about my girlfriend having an abortion. There were several other women besides her, but none of them ever got pregnant."

"Do you believe when you accepted Christ as your savior, He forgave your sins?"

"Yes."

"Part of accepting His forgiveness is forgiving yourself. His blood wiped your slate clean."

Forgiving myself? Brother Timothy's sermon from last Sunday. He'd heard it, but it hadn't sunk in. Maybe prayer time would help him embrace his clean slate.

"I think if you feel the call to be an associate pastor, you should answer that call. And your past could be a great testimony of the work God has done in you."

"I hadn't looked at it that way. I'll pray about it some more."

"I'll help you in the prayer department."

Lane stood and clasped the pastor's hand. "Thanks."

"No problem. Keep me posted. On Natalie and your calling."

Lane walked out of the office and headed toward his class.

Natalie. His steps stalled. Her slate had been wiped clean, too. Besides, she'd considered an abortion, but she hadn't gone through with it. And he knew from experience, if she'd really wanted to, she could have done it without ever telling Wyatt.

He owed her an apology. Even if he'd hurt her too badly for them to be together now, he owed her an apology.

"Hey." Clay stopped beside him. "Skipping class?"

"I was talking to Brother Timothy."

"Kendra was feeling sick, so I brought the truck around for Rayna to drive her home."

"Is she okay?"

"Goes with the territory. Rayna was sick a lot when she was pregnant. I don't know how women do it."

"Me, neither." Natalie had given birth to Hannah. Even though she hadn't really wanted to.

"By the way, we're having a trail ride at our place Thursday night if you wanna come."

"Will Natalie be there?"

"She's on the guest list, but I don't think Rayna's invited her yet. Do you want her there?"

"I do. In fact, if you don't mind, invite Wyatt, Hannah and Star. That way, she'll come for sure."

"They're actually on the list, too."

"Great. Count me in." Maybe by then, she'd have cooled off. Maybe she'd accept his apology. Maybe she could still be his.

If he hadn't hurt her too badly. Big oaf. He'd homed in on the one thing she probably most regretted in her life and condemned her for it. Without even listening to her side of the story. How could she want anything to do with him?

But he had to try.

Hannah would be at the trail ride. Natalie grabbed her keys. But Lane might be, too.

Maybe Kendra had intervened in Rayna's guest list and Lane wouldn't be there. But if he was there, could she face him? She had to. Spending time with Hannah would be worth it. And she wouldn't hide herself away again. Not because of Lane. Not because of anyone.

She paced the length of her kitchen and dining room.

But moving to Denton seemed like a good plan. Close to Hannah, farther from Lane. She'd already talked to Star about buying her house. And she'd talk to Wyatt about letting Hannah have her house. He and Star could even live there until Hannah grew up.

Wyatt living in her dollhouse? She laughed.

She hurried through the kitchen to the garage, jumped in her car, and started it. Halfway down the drive, she remembered the dress she'd bought Hannah from Caitlyn's store. Hannah's favorite color—pink—with lots of ribbons and lace. Hannah would love it.

Natalie braked. No sense in driving back to the garage. She hopped out of the car and hurried to the front door.

The dress lay on the kitchen table, right where she'd left it so she wouldn't forget it. Dress in hand, she stepped outside, locked the door and smoothed the see-through plastic bag over the fabric as she walked to her car.

A dog. Her feet stalled. A big dog right in front of her car. She dropped her keys.

The dog didn't move. No friendly tail wagging. But no growling either. It crouched low. In attack mode.

The memory surfaced. Long-ago jaws with sharp teeth clamped on her cheek. A chill crept through her.

Could she get back to the house? She'd locked the front door and she'd have to pick up her keys. The dog would catch up with her before she could get it unlocked. The garage door took a few seconds to slide up. Seconds she didn't have. She could run to the back fence. But could she get the latch open and the gate shut behind her before the dog caught up with her?

She took a step backward. The dog took a step toward her and barked.

A live oak stood two feet to her left with low branches she'd been meaning to have cut. She shot toward the tree, grabbed a limb and dragged herself up. The dog lunged at her from below, barking and snapping near her feet. She climbed to a higher limb.

"You stupid dog. This is my yard." Bravery from her perch. Big chicken. She dug her cell phone from her pocket. Daddy would rescue her.

But the phone was dead. As always, when she really needed it, she'd forgotten to charge it.

She climbed higher and the dog stopped lunging at her, but it still sat right below her, barking. Rusty chimed in from the backyard.

Maybe her parents or Caitlyn would hear the racket.

Just an hour or so of daylight left. The sun painted orange, pink and purple streaks across the sky. The June air was slightly cool. Perfect for the trail ride she wasn't going to. Would Wyatt wonder about her enough to come and check on her? Kendra would assume she hadn't shown up for fear that Lane would be there.

A bead of sweat trickled down the small of her back. How long would the dog stay? Would she have to spend the night in the tree?

Lane scanned the guests. No Natalie. He'd almost stopped by her place a dozen times this week, but decided to wait it out instead. Give her more time to cool down. What if she rejected him? That's what had kept him away. Coward.

But now Thursday night was here, and he was eager to see her. To attempt a reconciliation. Surely his harsh words couldn't kill love. And she'd said she loved him. Twice.

Kendra walked by, holding little Danielle's hand.

"Hey, Kendra, do you know if Nat's coming?"

She shrugged. "She's been a hermit this week. I talked to her on the phone and asked if she'd be here, but she didn't really say yes or no."

"I thought she was coming once she found out Hannah would be here." Wyatt, already astride his horse, looked toward Star and Hannah near the barn playing with a kitten. "I'm worried about her."

"Why?"

"She seemed upset this week. And she asked Star about buying our house in Denton. Something's not right with her."

Lane's chest went tight. To get away from him. She planned to slip quietly out of his life. Starting with avoiding him tonight.

"I'll go check on her." He bolted for his truck.

* * *

The dog wouldn't budge. Kept sitting there looking up at her like she was a big hunk of steak. At least the barking had stopped.

She straightened her back. Her muscles burned from having nothing to lean against.

Gravel crunched in her drive. Thank goodness. Maybe it was Caitlyn or her parents. A black truck came into view. Lane.

Her heart went into a frenzy. What was he doing here?

The dog watched the truck but didn't move or bark.

She could call out to him, look like a ninny sitting in a tree and have an awkward scene with him. Or she could keep quiet. He'd leave and she'd still be stuck here. She longed for rescue—but by anyone other than Lane.

His engine shut off and the truck door opened. The dog started barking again and bounded toward Lane.

Her insides twisted. "Lane, watch out."

He turned toward her voice, his gaze searching.

"The dog." She gestured wildly. "Get back in your truck."

He saw her. The dog caught up with him. "Hey there. Why, you're just a big pup." Lane stuck a hand toward the dog, palm up.

Natalie closed her eyes. She couldn't watch the dog maul Lane. She screamed.

"Natalie, it's okay. Look."

She opened her eyes. The dog lay belly up with Lane squatting above it, patting and murmuring.

"He's a puppy. He wanted to play with you."

"He's awfully big for a puppy."

"He's a German shepherd. Probably half grown. I think I've seen him down the road chasing cars. He probably gave a good chase and headed home, but saw you."

"Can you do something with him? My back is cramping."

"Sure." He opened his truck door. "Hop on up, pup. I'll take you home."

The dog jumped in and Lane shut the door.

Natalie covered her face and blew out a big sigh.

"How long you been up there?" Lane's voice was right beneath her.

"What time is it?" She climbed down a few limbs.

"Seven-thirty."

"I came out of the house at five till."

"Why didn't you call someone?"

"I forgot to charge my cell."

"Were you gonna stay up there all night?"

Her foot slid, but she caught herself with both hands and hung within jumping distance from the ground.

"Be careful. Let me help you." His hands settled on her waist from behind. "Let go, I've got you."

Her breath caught. If she argued with him, she'd probably start crying. She let go.

Lane held her until her feet hit the ground and she was steady.

She sidestepped him and stalked toward her car.

"Why are you so afraid of dogs?"

No escape. Lane was parked behind her. "When I was little, we were at my grandparents'. I petted their dog, but I didn't know he had a sore ear. He bit me, right on the cheek."

"Ouch."

"Yeah. Okay, so you rescued me and I appreciate it, but you can go now."

"I'll always protect you, Nat. If you'll let me."

Her mouth went dry. "I want to get to the trail ride."

"They've probably left by now."

"Were you there?"

He nodded. "Wyatt said you were coming. When you didn't, I figured it was because of me."

"Hannah was expecting me. I need to go."

"If you'll hold up, I'll go with you, help you catch up with them and then leave."

"And leave me alone?"

"If you'll talk to me."

"About?"

"Let's sit." He gestured toward the porch.

Not trusting her shaky legs with the steps, Natalie perched on the bottom one.

Lane settled beside her. "I'm sorry for judging you. I had no right."

"It doesn't matter."

"Yes, it does. Please forgive me." His elbow touched hers. "Tell me—why didn't you abort Hannah?"

The air went out of her lungs. She swallowed hard. "Wyatt wouldn't let me rest until I agreed to have her."

"But you could have just done it and never told him. Or you could have done it secretly and broken all ties with him. He'd have had to leave you alone after that. Did you want an abortion?"

Chapter 13

Pressure built in Natalie's chest. "No." Her voice cracked. "I was scared and I wanted out, but I didn't want to kill her. I latched on to Wyatt's offer to take her to get out from under the responsibility." The pressure burst like a bubble leaving her almost weak. She hadn't wanted to kill Hannah.

"I think if Wyatt hadn't taken her, you'd have done the right thing."

Me, too. "Thanks for helping me realize it." Her voice came out barely a whisper.

"I wanted to tell you something." He sucked in a deep breath. "Something that will change my life."

Was he leaving town? Going back on the rodeo circuit? "What's that?"

"God's been after me to do something. I wasn't sure what, at first. I think He wants me to be an associate pastor. I'm starting seminary next semester."

Her insides reeled. "Really? Wow."

"Yeah. Who'd have ever thought? Me, preaching?"

"I think it's awesome."

"I was hoping you would." He took her hand in his. "I need you by my side, Nat. I've tried to make a life without you for over nine years. And it hasn't worked."

Nine years of hurting each other. He didn't need her on this new venture. Natalie Wentworth, a preacher's wife? What was she thinking? Lane hadn't even mentioned marriage.

Natalie tugged her hand out of his grasp. "I don't know if I'm God's idea of a support system for a preacher."

"If He wants me, I think He'll take you. Our slates are wiped clean."

"Huh?"

"I talked to Brother Timothy about not feeling worthy of being a preacher. He reminded me that Jesus' blood wiped my slate clean. Yours is clean, too. Come on, Nat, give us a chance."

She stood. "I think we've hurt each other too much. Maybe we should go our separate ways."

"We tried that. And I don't know about you, but I've been miserable."

"We've been miserable together, too."

"But we can start fresh."

"I don't think there's anything left to start fresh with." She turned toward the house. "I'm moving to Denton."

"That's not far."

"I need to concentrate on Hannah. Not you."

"I thought I was following you to the trail ride."

"I'll call and tell Wyatt what happened. He'll probably bring Hannah by on the way home." She went inside and shut the door. Tears scalded her eyes. How could she let him go? But with constant human reminders from her past, how could she be a pastor's wife? He needed to start over with someone new. Pursue his new dream with someone else. Someone with a slate Jesus didn't need to clean quite so much.

A knock sounded at Natalie's door. She wiped her eyes. Maybe a visit with Hannah would cheer her up. She scooped the dress up and hid it behind her back, then hurried to the door.

Kendra stood on her porch with her hands propped on her hips. "What are you doing?"

"Waiting for Wyatt to bring Hannah by. He agreed to, since I didn't make the trail ride and I have a gift for her." She held the dress up. "What are you doing here?"

"I was worried about you. Why didn't you make the trail ride?"

"It's a long story."

"Did I hear something about you moving to Denton?"

She stiffened. "I need to focus on Hannah."

"And to get away from Lane?"

"I think I could focus more that way."

Kendra sighed. "Don't run away from love, Natalie."

"I'm not."

"You sure about that?"

"What if Lane and I aren't supposed to be together? What if God has someone else for each of us? Someone with no past history. Uncomplicated." But even as she said the words, she couldn't imagine loving anyone else.

"I haven't known you that long, but I can't imagine you with anyone other than Lane."

Was there an echo in here, capturing her thoughts?

"Why would God put love in your hearts for each other if He didn't want you together?"

"I'm scared."

"Of?"

"Of loving him so much. What if it doesn't work out? I'm not sure I could deal with losing him again."

"You've got God on your side this time. As long as you keep Him first, you'll be fine."

"I don't think I'm pastor's wife material."

"What?"

"Lane's going to seminary next semester to be an associate pastor."

"I'm not youth director's wife material. But God makes all things new. Look at me. Look at the apostle Paul."

Kendra's past wasn't quite as tarnished as Natalie's. But Stetson and Kendra were sold out for the youth and making a difference in young lives.

"I've never prayed for someone before as diligently as I have for you." Kendra gave her a hug. "God's on the verge of putting His plan for you in place. Don't mess it up."

"You're a great friend."

A crunch of gravel and headlights appeared down the drive.

"That's probably Wyatt with Hannah." Kendra pulled away and headed down the steps. "Just think about what I said. Pray about it."

"I will."

Could she and Lane make it together with all their past complications and hurts? Could they become something new and work for the Lord together? *Is this what I want or what You want, Lord?*

Peace flowed through her. A peace she'd only known once before. When she'd given her heart to Jesus.

"Is this a sign, Lord? I need a sign."

Maybe it was Lane driving up. *Lord, if You want us together, let Lane show up here.*

She held her breath as a dark truck braked to let Kendra back her car out, then rolled to a stop. The driver's side door opened. Wyatt stepped out, then opened the back door to get Hannah out of her car seat.

Natalie's breath came out in a rush.

Forget Lane. Focus on Hannah.

Lane unloaded the white vinyl fence railing. Just like the fence he'd built in the back. Natalie wouldn't have to worry about dogs or overzealous pups anymore. And she'd know he wasn't going anywhere. He'd let her down three times—in high school, by inferring she might wreck Wyatt's marriage and by condemning her for considering an abortion. But he wouldn't let her down again. Natalie Wentworth would know she could count on him. He'd prove it to her.

"What are you doing?"

He whirled around to find her standing on the porch, barefoot, wearing a black business suit.

"I'm building a fence around your house."

"Why?"

"You should be able to get to your car without a dog keeping you from it."

She seemed shaky, fluttery. "I have a garage."

"That didn't help last time."

"I forgot something and went back inside. Next time, I'll drive back in and close the garage door."

"But you shouldn't have to. I want you to feel safe in your own yard."

"I really appreciate it. But I'm thinking about deeding this place over to Hannah and letting Wyatt and Star live here until she grows up."

"I'll build the fence either way, so Hannah can be safe in her own yard."

Her smile went all the way to her eyes.

Touchdown. Hopefully straight to her heart. "I'm putting an automatic gate at the end of the drive, too."

She propped her hands on her hips. "Don't you think that's a bit much?"

"Not for you."

Natalie's throat convulsed. She looked away from him and scanned the yard again. "Why are you doing this?"

"To keep you and Hannah safe."

"Let me get my shoes on." She disappeared inside the house.

Minutes later, she strode out. High heels made her legs look even longer. The prim business suit feminized by a red concoction of lace and silk that took his breath away. Her calves were bare under her knee-length skirt. No panty hose in sight.

"You look awfully businessy. Got a meeting?"

"I meet with the heads of all the businesses at the Stockyards this morning. We're finalizing my publicity plan today." She checked her watch and plopped onto the tailgate of his truck.

Lane's jaw dropped.

He settled beside her and the tailgate dipped with his weight.

She didn't move away from him. Her lips were only inches away.

It took everything he had not to claim them. "Shouldn't you be fluttering off to work? Getting away from me as quick as you can?"

"My meeting's in an hour and a half, and I'd rather stay."

"You would?" His brain couldn't catch up with what was going on.

"I love you, Lane. I always have."

His heart raced. "And I love you. So what's keeping us apart?"

"Nothing."

"Nothing?" He leaned closer to her. Their arms touched. She didn't move away.

"I was scared, okay? Scared of loving you so much and it not working out. Scared of your calling."

He swallowed hard. "That makes two of us. I'm scared, too. Especially of losing you."

"I turned my fear over to God last night." She leaned her forehead against Lane's. "Will you marry me?"

"Whoa. That was a quick turnaround." He pulled her into his arms.

"I prayed about you, and God gave me peace. Then just to make sure, I asked for God to give me a sign. For you to show up here."

He grinned. "Really?"

"And sure enough, you show up this morning being all sweet and building me another fence. For Hannah. I'm pretty sure God deals in flashing arrow signs."

His gaze locked with hers. "Natalie Wentworth, I love you. But I can't accept your proposal."

Her breath caught. "Why not?"

"Because I'm not that kind of guy."

Her eyes got too shiny.

Natalie blinked, pushed away from him and slid off the tailgate. She faced him, but kept her gaze in the vicinity of his throat. "Well, I won't do anything else. I'm not that type of girl. Anymore."

Lane caught her chin with gentle fingers and forced her gaze to meet his. "That's not what I meant. I plan on marrying you. But I'll do the proposing. On my timeline. I don't even have a ring yet."

"Oh." Her voice went all breathy.

"I wanna do this right. You need to meet my mom. I need to ask your daddy for your hand and the whole shebang. But be ready. I won't wait long." He stood and his gaze settled on her lips.

His lips caught hers. His knees went weak. He was putty in her embrace.

Lane groaned and pulled away. "Not very long at all. Be ready with the right answer for me."

"I will," she said, her voice low with anticipation.

"Now." He turned her toward her car. "I better get busy on this fence and you better get to Fort Worth. Don't want to be late for your meeting."

She checked her watch. "Oh, my! I have to go. That is, if my legs will hold me up."

Lane chuckled. "Same here."

Thank You, Lord, for working everything out with Natalie. Lane squeezed her hand as they approached the huge house. He'd forgotten how large her folks' house was. Even larger than Natalie's.

"Do you mind if we live in my farmhouse? I mean—after I propose and we get married, that is."

"I'd love to live in your house." She smiled up at him and his heart did a two-step.

"It's an old fixer-upper, but I don't think I could live in that dollhouse of yours. Seems like a great plan to give it to Hannah and let Wyatt and Star live there." He swung her hand in a wide arch, giddy with life in general.

"To tell you the truth, I never really wanted a dollhouse. A fixer-upper farmhouse sounds great to me. My interior-decorator cousin could help us remodel."

"As long as it's not too feminine."

"It can't stay a bachelor pad. Not if I'm going to live there."

"We'll work it out. I've got two spare bedrooms. But if we want more than one child, we'll need more, so Hannah can have her own room when she visits. And if you want a newer house, we can look into that, too. Whatever makes you happy."

"You make me happy." But the light was missing from her eyes.

"Something's bothering you."

"Do you think your mom liked me?" Her tone sounded unsure.

"She's been that way since my dad left when I was fifteen. Won't let anybody near. Not even me, but I wanted you to meet her. To do things right."

"She seems so sad."

"She is. She's mad at God for my dad leaving. I've been praying for her and inviting her to church."

"I'll pray for her, too."

As they stepped up on the porch, he pulled her into his arms, unable to resist those lips a second longer. Sparks flew and his brain stalled.

"Ahem."

Natalie jerked away from him.

Her dad glowered at Lane. "Hello again."

"Hi, Daddy. You remember Lane." Natalie's voice quivered.

"Nice to see you again, sir." Lane offered his hand.

Daniel ignored it. "Come on in. Dinner's almost ready. Don't want it to get cold while you stand on *my* porch kissing *my* daughter."

Lane's heart sank. The evening hadn't started off well. He'd have to spend the rest of the night on his best behavior and win her dad over. His future depended on it. He trailed behind Natalie as they entered the house, which was decorated in shimmering fabrics with creamy tones similar to Natalie's living room.

"Tell me, Lane, any fans of Zane Grey in your family?"

"Actually, my dad was a big Lane Frost fan, from his high school career on."

"You can't be all bad, then."

"Daddy!"

"Are you a hunting man, Lane?"

"I used to go hunting with my dad. But not since I was a teenager. My parents divorced and…" He hadn't seen his dad much since.

Daniel's scowl grew deeper. Apparently divorce was a bad word in the Wentworth household. Two strikes against him—couldn't keep his lips to himself and a long line of divorce ran in his family.

"Ever been on a wild boar hunt?"

"No, sir."

"I'm leaving for a hunt Wednesday after evening Bible study. Just a few hours away over in Centerville. Staying until Friday afternoon. Why don't you come with me? From what I gather, you only work on weekends. We can get to know each other. Male bonding time."

Daniel had checked him out. Enough to know what he did for a living. Hmm.

"I don't know, Daddy. Lane may not want to."

"It sounds like fun." Lane tried to sound convincing. Wild boars on the loose and a man who didn't like him with a loaded gun. What could be more fun than that? The perfect place to ask the man with the gun if Lane could marry his daughter.

Natalie shot him a worried look. She was worth it.

Lane's back ached from leaning against nothing, perched on a tiny platform high in a tree just after daylight. Daniel Wentworth sat beside him, relaxed, reclining against the tree trunk.

The boars ran loose and wild. They'd already seen a whole herd, but the animals never stopped as they ran past and down the other side of a knoll out of range.

At least he was in a tree. Now all Lane had to worry about was the man with the rifle.

"Tell me about yourself, Lane," Daniel whispered. "How long have you known Natalie?"

"Since middle school, sir."

"I see. What about your family?"

Lane sucked in a deep breath. Would the specter of his parents' divorce keep him from Natalie? "My mom lives in Denton. We used to have a farm in Aubrey, but after my parents divorced, my mom got an apartment. She still lives there. My dad moved to Oklahoma."

"See him much?"

"No, sir." Lane sighed. "He remarried. Had more kids. They're a lot younger than me. I used to go visit. But his wife didn't like me and the other kids were jealous of me. Just seemed easier not to."

"Divorce is a tough thing."

"Yes, sir. I promised myself—a long time ago—it would never happen to me."

"So you've never been married?"

"No, sir." Avoided divorce for a long time by not letting himself love. But Natalie had broken his rules. "When I marry, it'll be for keeps."

"Claire and I have thirty years in."

"Congratulations."

"Hasn't been easy." Daniel closed his eyes for a second. "Especially the early years. We never had financial concerns, but money doesn't buy happiness. Claire had issues. I had issues. Humans have issues. It's learning to deal with your issues together. That's the key."

"Yes, sir."

"Has Natalie told you about her missing aunt?"

"No, sir."

"Claire and I had only been married a few months when her younger sister, Millie, disappeared. Only sixteen years old—vanished."

"Did they find her?"

"Not a trace. The police treated it like a kidnapping, but got reports she ran off with her boyfriend. But thirty years later, you'd think she'd have come back by now if that was the case."

"I can't imagine how your wife must feel."

"It made her real overprotective of the girls. Caitlyn was always the easy one. Did what we told her. Never caused any problems. Our rule follower."

He shook his head. "But Natalie—she was always stubborn. Wanted to make her own rules and break everyone else's."

"She ran into some jerk in high school. He…mistreated her and she went wild. I thought Claire would go nuts. She was terrified Natalie would wind up missing like Millie."

Lane's stomach churned. If only Daniel knew he was talking to the jerk.

"Her mother and I didn't know what to do, so we got her in church. We all met the Lord, except Natalie. It didn't take with her. Things got better for Claire and me, but eventually things got so bad with Natalie, I said things I didn't mean and she left. I didn't see her for over two years. Not until a few months ago. She's straightening her life out now. Letting the Lord lead."

He'd not only caused Natalie pain, but her whole family had suffered because of him.

"I'm glad Natalie found the Lord."

"You a Christian, Lane?"

"Yes, sir. A newbie. Got saved nine months ago."

"That's good."

Finally, he'd done something right. And Nat's mom liked him. Maybe he could build on that.

Lane closed his eyes. Just spit it out. "Sir, I'd like your permission to marry her."

"I see." Daniel swallowed hard as if he'd choked on a bitter pill.

"But before you answer—" Lane sucked in a deep breath "—there's something you need to know about me."

"What's that?"

"That jerk she encountered in high school." He sighed. "That would be me."

Daniel cocked the 30-30 rifle he held.

Lane gasped.

A blast rang through his head.

Chapter 14

"Got him!" Daniel whooped.

High-pitched squeals echoed through the woods.

Lane followed Daniel's gaze. A huge boar wallowed in tall grass twenty feet away, then went still.

"Sir, did you hear what I said?"

"I did. I heard it back when it happened."

"You knew? Back then?"

"I wanted to know if you'd come clean with me. Especially while I held a loaded gun."

"I'm sorry, sir."

"You should be."

"My parents divorced and I went on a rampage. Natalie happened to get in my way and got burned."

"Yes, she did."

"I imagine you want me out of her life, for me to leave her alone."

"If I had my druthers."

"But I can't do that, sir. I love her. I loved her back then. I was just too young and stupid to admit it."

"Seems you've got one option."

"What's that?"

"Marry her and spend the rest of your life treating her right."

"I'd love that chance, sir."

"Then do it." Daniel climbed down from the stand. "Let's go see about that hog. Think I'll have him stuffed."

Lane clambered down after him. "Sir, I won't let you down."

"You better not. Hurt my girl again and you'll answer to me and my 30-30." Daniel clapped him on the back so hard his teeth rattled. "You know, I always thought if you wanted to hide a body, out here would be a great place."

"Sir, I'll treat Natalie right, but it won't be because I'm afraid of you."

Daniel stopped and turned to face him. The rifle rested on his shoulder. "Is that so?"

"I'll treat her right because I love her. I respect her and I want to honor her. I made mistakes with her in the past. But this time, I haven't done anything but kiss her. And I won't, not until we're married."

Daniel smiled. "Music to a dad's ears. You might be worth knowing, after all."

"And one other thing, I intend to provide for her. I'm starting seminary this fall to answer the call as associate pastor, but I make good money as a rodeo pickup man and I've started my own fencing company."

"A preacher, huh?" Daniel slung his arm over Lane's shoulder. "Congratulations."

"Thank you, sir. I'm also planning to turn my farm into a ranch over the next few years. I've already bought some cattle and I don't want to live in Natalie's house. I'd feel like a kept man if I moved into my wife's house, and I fully support Nat signing it over to Hannah."

"Have you discussed this with Natalie?"

"Yes, sir. The only thing I haven't discussed with her is—I don't know what kind of money Natalie has, but I want to sign a prenup. I'm not interested in her money, and I'd like to prove it with a legal document. She'll fight me on it, so if we could keep that between us, life will be more peaceful."

"But you don't have to prove anything to me. You already have."

"If it's all the same to you, sir, I'd like to make it legal." Lane pushed a limb out of the way and held it until Daniel passed through the opening.

The pig trail narrowed. Dead leaves from last fall crunched and twigs snapped as they made their way through the brush. At least Lane hoped it was the two of them making all the noise and not a herd of pigs on their trail.

"Tell you what. I've made a mint with real estate and longhorns. Natalie has a trust she's entitled to when she turns thirty-five. I'll have my lawyer draw up a prenup on that."

"Along with whatever she inherits from you. I'd appreciate it, sir."

Daniel clapped him on the back again. Gentler this time. "You have my blessing."

"Thank you, sir."

"Let's haul in the kill, get some lunch and then we'll see if you can take down a boar. I always donate the meat to the children's home and they can always use more food."

Lane smiled and fell in behind his future father-in-law as the trail narrowed even more. He liked this man. Terrorizing his daughter's suitor with a rifle one minute, worrying about parentless children the next.

* * *

Natalie hurried to Lane's door. He'd begged off on supper before the rodeo. Would he propose tonight? Over a nice candlelight dinner.

He'd said he had a surprise for her at his house. A ring? Didn't he know the way he made her feel? He should realize it was dangerous to propose to her anywhere near a bed.

The door swung open before she could knock.

"Hey, beautiful." His smile melted her into a puddle at his feet.

"How did the hunting trip go?"

"Fine." He drew her into his arms.

"Fine?" That's all? "You and Daddy got along okay?"

"Fine. We each killed a boar."

Did you ask him if you could marry me?

"Come on upstairs, and let me show you what I've been up to. Then it's out the door for you before I'm tempted to never let you go."

Upstairs?

She climbed the stairs with him following. Usually only bedrooms were upstairs. But she trusted him. Just not herself so much.

"No peeking." His hands clamped over her eyes as they reached the top.

Her hands covered his. With his chest pressed against her back, he walked her forward. His nearness sent a shiver through her.

"Ready."

"Mmm-hmm."

"Don't worry. I'm not trying to pull anything." He moved his hands. "Open your eyes."

It was a bedroom. Pink froufrou with ruffles and lace everywhere—the canopy, the bedspread and the curtains. Definitely not Lane's bedroom.

"What is this?"

"For Hannah. Think she'll like it?"

Natalie gasped.

"What? She likes pink, doesn't she? I don't mean for her to live with us, but when she visits, I figured she ought to have her own room. So I got Jenna's number from your mom and had her tackle decorating while I was gone with your dad on the hunt. Is it too fancy?"

"It's perfect." Her voice came out in a whisper.

"What's wrong?"

"You'll never know what this means to me." She leaned back against him. "You're welcoming my daughter into your home."

"Our home. Our daughter." He turned her into his arms. "You sure you'll be happy moving out of your dollhouse and into this fixer-upper?"

"I'll be happy wherever you are." She pressed her cheek against his chest, treasuring every heartbeat.

"I could stay like this all night. But I've got a rodeo to work. We better get going."

No proposal. It would come. She knew it. But waiting was not her best event.

Nerves danced through Natalie as she neared her usual seat by Kendra at the Cowtown Coliseum. Lacie and Star sat on the other side of her friend. Apparently Kendra had gotten over her unease where Star was concerned.

Lane hadn't opened up any more about the hunting trip with her dad. And, apparently, she wouldn't get her proposal tonight.

She loved Lane. He loved her. What was he waiting for? He'd had time to get a ring and time to talk to her father.

Her stomach took a dive. If Daddy didn't approve, would Lane still propose to her?

Of course he would. He'd fixed up a room for Hannah. But if Daddy was being stubborn, he could delay things.

"Hey." Kendra frowned at her. "You okay? You seem jumpy. You and Lane are okay now, right?"

"We're fine." *I think.* "How are you feeling?"

Kendra patted her protruding stomach. "Like a cow. Danielle even compared me to one. But other than that, fine."

Natalie laughed. "You can always depend on children to say what they think. What does Danielle think of the new baby coming?"

"She's excited and I'm so thankful. I was afraid she'd be jealous."

Replaced by a biological baby. It could happen to Hannah someday.

"Can I ask you something?" Natalie whispered.

"Sure."

"What if Star and Wyatt have other kids? Do you think Star will love Hannah less than her own children?"

"I can only speak for me." Kendra shook her head. "I love Danielle just as much as I love this new baby. She's mine as surely as if I'd given birth to her myself. And I imagine Star will feel the same way. It's obvious how much she loves Hannah."

The engine roared to life and the huge tractor in the center of the arena signaled the beginning of the rodeo. As the tractor cleared the gate, "We Are the Champions" blared over the speakers, Quinn made a few announcements and the arena went black. The "Star-Spangled Banner" began playing and a spotlight shone on a girl singing it in the middle of the arena. As the patriotic anthem ended, she launched into a popular country song.

Natalie's mind went back to Lane. What had Daddy said to him? Where was her proposal?

The song ended and the girl left the arena. It went dark again.

"Ladies and gentlemen, tonight before we get started, we have a special guest with an important question." Quinn's voice bounced around the arena. "Cowtown Coliseum's very own pickup man extraordinaire, Lane Gray."

The spotlight shone on Lane in the middle of the arena. Feminine whistles and whoops echoed around her.

What was he doing?

He dropped to one knee.

Her heart jolted.

"I've loved Natalie Wentworth since high school, but I made some mistakes and ruined her reputation. We went our separate ways on destructive paths. But God got hold of us and we're both Christians now. We've started over on a new path and embraced purity."

A smattering of applause echoed through the crowd.

"So tonight, I have a very important question for the most beautiful, special woman I've ever known. I love you, Natalie Wentworth. Will you marry me?"

As she clutched a hand to her heart, a second spotlight blinded her.

The crowd began to chant. "Yes, yes, yes, yes."

Her vision blurred and she nodded her head.

Lane shot her a grin meant only for her despite the chaos surrounding them. He tipped his hat. "See you after the rodeo."

The arena went dark again and the spotlight veered away from her and spun in dizzying circles around the stands as the crowd cheered.

Kendra hugged her. "Congratulations."

Her stomach did giddy somersaults. "I can't believe I have to wait until after the rodeo to see him."

"Anticipation. I think he planned it that way."

"Did you know about this?"

"If you didn't sit in your usual spot, I was supposed to track you down."

"Well, I can't wait." Natalie hurried toward the chutes where the staff gathered before the rodeo, while the rodeo queen rounded the arena with her flag.

Lane saw Natalie and hopped off the fence to meet her. His arms came around her and their lips met.

Fireworks went off in her head and heart.

Lane pulled away. "Whew. Keep that up and nobody's gonna believe the purity thing."

Stetson tugged on Lane's arm. "Sorry to interrupt, but, Lane, you gotta get in the arena."

He let go of her and backed away.

Weak-kneed, Natalie watched him go. "I love you. Be careful. Mind on the broncs and bulls."

"A challenge." He winked and turned away from her.

Lane blew out a big breath and scanned the crowd milling about before the wedding. A mere five months had passed since he'd bumped into Natalie at Quinn and Lacie's wedding. Now it was almost time for their own.

There were right around one hundred and fifty guests. Natalie had gotten her wish—a big, splashy August wedding at the Ever After Chapel filled to capacity. If it had been left up to him, he'd have taken the sneak-off-and-elope route. Or had a tiny gathering of close family and friends in a barn.

The Ever After Chapel? He would have thought she'd think it was too rustic. Too cheesy. But deep down, underneath her ultramodern persona, she was an old-fashioned, traditional kind of gal.

And this was Nat's day. Whatever it took to make her happy, he'd do. Even wear an albino penguin suit. He shook his head at the getup he wore.

But he'd won on the honeymoon. A week at a Florida beach to beat the Texas heat wave.

Of course, if he had his way, they'd barely see the beach. He grinned. Natalie all to himself. Finally. With God's blessing. And her father's.

And they'd be back in plenty of time for Hannah's second birthday. Life was good.

Wyatt sat near one of the windows in the rustic old chapel with an empty spot for Star beside him. Lane checked his watch—five minutes until showtime.

He strode over to Wyatt. "I wanted to talk to you."

"Sure. Have a seat." Wyatt had mellowed during the last several months. He was no longer combative and overly protective since he and Natalie had come to an agreement about Hannah.

"I just want you to know, I love Hannah. She's a doll and I plan on being an attentive stepdad and treating her right, but I won't try to be her dad. She has a dad."

"I appreciate that. Natalie told me about the room you set up for her."

"I think we're all gonna be fine, and Hannah has lots of folks to love her. I appreciate you letting me in her life. She's a special little girl."

"You ready to get this show on the road?" Clay stood at the end of the pew.

"Past ready." Lane followed his best man to the front of the church.

"You nervous?"

"Not at all." Finally, he was marrying the woman he'd loved since high school. What was there to be nervous about?

As he took his place by Brother Timothy, Clay and his groomsman, Quinn, the traditional wedding march began. Who'd have thought Natalie would be so traditional? His soon-to-be bride was full of surprises. Kept him guessing and on his toes. He liked it that way. Life with Natalie Gray would never be dull.

Hannah strewed red rose petals as she made her way toward him. Soft laughter swept through the guests as Max, Lacie's son, carried the pillow with the rings under his arm. Good thing the rings were tied in place. Bridesmaid Kendra was next. Eight months pregnant.

He could picture Natalie that way. Carrying his baby.

Maid of honor Caitlyn followed. They both took way too long to mosey down the aisle.

The music intensified and the double doors in the back opened. Natalie was a vision in white lace. His breath stalled.

Natalie scanned the rustic white wood walls that arched at the corners into the ceiling, the primitive wood pews and the aged wood trim and accents of the Ever After Chapel as she stood just outside the slightly open double glass doors. From the time an older cousin had gotten married here when Natalie was nine, she'd dreamed of having her wedding here. She knew Mama would have chosen somewhere fancier, but she hadn't argued.

Caitlyn and Kendra took their places at the front of the church. The doors swung open wide and Natalie's gaze locked with Lane's.

If she'd been wearing socks, he'd have knocked them clean off. He was dazzling in his white tux with tails and a red cummerbund to match her rose bouquet. She'd initially planned an off-white dress, but Lane had reminded her that in God's eyes they were innocent. And God's eyes were the only eyes that mattered. Other than Lane's.

Daddy nudged her. "Ready?"

Gripping his arm tighter, she nodded.

As she took slow, measured stutter-steps up the aisle, Lane's gaze never left hers. She stole a quick glance at Hannah, her hair curled and tied with a red ribbon, playing with a few petals still in her basket. Natalie smiled and focused on her soon-to-be husband again.

Her life had been such a mess when she'd returned to Aubrey and crashed that wedding. But now the two people she loved most in the world were hers. *Thank You, Lord.*

Lane's smile promised happily ever after. Something she'd forgotten she'd ever wanted—until the cowboy of her high school dreams sauntered back into her life.

She took the final step and stopped beside him. Daddy handed her over to Lane and went to sit with Mama.

Lane's hand closed over hers. Lane, rock solid beside her, for as long as they both lived. The cowboy who'd claimed the jagged pieces of her heart and put them back together. Her first and only love rekindled, strong enough to blot out a lifetime of rodeo regrets.

Her throat clogged and his handsome face blurred.

The music stopped. Lane squeezed her hand and shot her a wink—filled with promises of forever.

* * * * *